Secrets of Sugarcreek
✚

a STRANGER for

Christmas

Secrets of Sugarcreek

✝

a STRANGER *for*

Christmas

SERENA B. MILLER

Edited by
HANNAH MILLER

LJ EMORY
PUBLISHING

Cover & Interior design by Jacob Miller

Published by L. J. Emory Publishing

First L. J. Emory Publishing trade paperback edition February 2025

ISBN 978-1-940283-67-8

ISBN 978-1-940283-68-5 (eBook Version)

To Rhoda and Freeman Mullet,
owners of The Gospel Shop of Sugarcreek,
who have spent their lives encouraging Christian
writers, while providing excellent reading material
for the beautiful village of Sugarcreek, Ohio.

*"For where your treasure is,
there will your heart be also."*

~Matthew 6:21

PROLOGUE

My earliest childhood memories are of falling asleep curled up in the corner of a bar while my mother, Desiree Stanton, sang her heart out for people who were too busy drinking and talking to pay attention.

While other little girls enjoyed helping pick out their supplies for the first day of school, I worried about if we'd have enough money for food. Having the correct crayons was way less important to me than going hungry.

Mom usually managed to keep the two of us fed, though. When she didn't have work as a singer or an actor, she earned money by waitressing. At least, that's what she told me, although I don't remember ever seeing her work in a restaurant. There were, however, many boyfriends who had plenty of money in their pockets. She never bothered with any man who didn't.

There were also acting lessons when she could afford them. Sometimes if there was no one available to babysit, she toted me around with her to auditions. Mom had dreams of becoming famous.

Then suddenly, she was.

Desiree's big break was a minor role in a movie with a brilliant director. It caught people's attention. A juicier supporting role came along on the heels of that minor success. Eventually, she received an Emmy nomination for a daytime TV drama. After that, the offers came pouring in.

While her dream turned into reality, we both had to learn how to live with it. As her fame grew, I watched her deal with rude fans, mentally ill stalkers, and survive five broken marriages.

One of those marriages produced the best stepfather a little girl could ever wish for. Rick Downey was my mom's third husband. He was also an extraordinarily kind person. We were best buddies for six years while Desiree went from one movie location to another, with only brief intervals at home.

I was twelve when she divorced him. It was shattering. In my grief, I told her I hated her and liked Rick better. That was a mistake. From that moment on, she made certain I never saw him again. My heartbreak as a twelve-year-old was a big part of what she and I have today —a very complicated mother/daughter relationship. Rarely do I know where Desiree is in the world. Like a nervous butterfly, she flits into my life at random times, dispenses advice, and then disappears.

Because of my mother's life choices, I have never hungered for fame. I grew up knowing the reality and the toll it can take all too well. And so, as an adult, I became a ghost. Not literally, of course, but professionally.

This is what I do: I watch and take notes as famous people live their lives. Then I research, get inside their heads, and help them "write" their autobiographies.

An M.A. in literature from Columbia University, and a total immunity to being impressed by overachievers, makes it a perfect fit. Plus, I have a visceral understanding of the challenges celebrities face. It is one benefit of growing up with Desiree Stanton for a mother. Another benefit is that my mother's fame helped get me started. Even though I was only in my twenties when I started writing professionally, a few words from her and the doors popped open.

My first ghost-written book became a bestseller—more because of the racy content than my skill as a writer. A famous actress, a virtual recluse, decided in her late nineties to "tell all." Mom suggested to her that I write her story.

That actress named names and told stories and exhibited the value of outliving all one's colleagues, because no one was still left alive to call her a liar. Authoring that book was enormous fun, and it paid a lot better than the few fiction books I had published.

My present project is a book with Ezekiel Cross, better known by his fans and friends as E.C. Sometimes they call him Crossfire, which is the name of his band. He is a rapper from Detroit who lost a beloved younger brother to gang violence.

Some people refer to him as a Christian rapper, but he does not speak about himself in those terms. He says he is a rapper who is also a Christian. Ezekiel has a gift of getting through to kids reared in situations that make them feel hopeless. He has quite a following, and I'm happy to do what I can to help with that.

CHAPTER 1

I t was the second day of April, and I was listening to a clueless hotel manager try to talk Ezekiel Cross into accepting the hotel's fancy labeled brand of purified bottled water. The manager was a nervous little man who clearly didn't know how to read a room or his famous guest. Several weeks earlier, Ezekiel had requested a specific brand of bottled spring water, but it still hadn't arrived. E.C. was bone-tired and growing frustrated.

It was six in the morning, and we had just arrived at the hotel from LaGuardia on a red-eye flight after a two-month, thirty-city tour that started in Dallas and ended here in New York City. The last concert was later that night, a benefit for special needs children. E.C. was donating all the money he earned back to the charity.

In my opinion, the rapper had earned the right to have his favorite water in his hotel suite. I glanced out the tall window down at Central Park, where an early spring sunrise was setting the park ablaze. I wished I were down there instead of standing in that eleventh-floor hotel suite, listening to E.C. and the hotel manager argue about water while E.C.'s entourage milled about.

From what I could gather, the manager was proud that his hotel had their own designer label water. I'd been on tour with E.C. and his people for the last two weeks, and I was more than ready to tuck myself into my Manhattan apartment and not talk to anyone for a few days.

E.C. held the hotel's bottle of water up, pointing to the label. "Your water is purified with reverse osmosis," he said.

"So?" the manager replied.

"It has no minerals in it," E.C. explained, pacing. His favorite purple dressing robe billowed behind him, and his long, dark dreadlocks cascaded down the front. He looked exactly like one would expect rapper royalty from Detroit to look—which was the point.

"Water with no natural minerals pulls minerals from the body," he added, carefully enunciating every word. On tour, depending on who he was communicating with, I'd heard him switch to inner-city street speech so thick and fast it was hard to follow. But for the hotel manager, he was using what I'd privately started thinking of as his "professor" voice.

The conversation about bottled water was getting on my sleep-deprived nerves, so I turned away from the window and stepped in.

"Here's the deal," I said, locking eyes with the hotel manager. "If E.C. drinks too much purified water, it can cause dehydration. Dehydration can affect his voice. He has a benefit concert tonight for special needs children. Around eight thousand people will be disappointed if he can't perform. And if that happens, I plan to make sure E.C.'s 3.2 million online fans know that the reason the concert was canceled is because this hotel could not provide the hydration he requested."

The manager considered the ramifications of that for a beat. "I'll see what I can do," he said before hurrying from the room.

"Thanks." E.C. sank into a gray suede chair with a high back. "Where'd you learn to scare people like that?"

I shrugged. "My mother never met a hotel manager she couldn't intimidate."

He gave me a look, clearly trying to remember who I was. I saved him the trouble. "Amy Stanton. I'm your new ghostwriter."

E.C. focused on me for the first time since I'd signed up to write his life story. "You're not the writer I started the tour with. What happened to her?"

"She quit."

"Was it something I did?" He sounded genuinely concerned.

"No. The tour wore her out. She said she was going to stay at home and write children's books from now on."

"Can't say I blame her." He placed both hands on his lower back and stretched. I heard his back crack. "So, you and me, are we starting from scratch?"

"No. I've already done the basic research, but we still need to talk. Preferably without an army of people listening."

He waved toward the door. "Everybody out!"

I watched as his "people" slowly filed out into the hallway. We were all tired, but E.C. looked the worst. He seemed older than when the tour started. On stage, he performed with the energy and passion of a twenty-year-old, but at the end of this thirty-city tour, he looked every one of his forty-eight years. He'd been performing for over twenty-five years and somewhere in his home back in Detroit, he had a stash of prestigious awards.

"Go ahead, ask me your questions," he said, his voice heavy with exhaustion.

I shook my head. "I've already set up several appointments with you through your manager. You need to get some rest before the concert tonight, E.C."

Relief flashed across his face as he leaned back, closing his eyes. "Do you like rap music, Amy?"

"Not at all," I said, shouldering my purse. "Never did. Probably never will. But the people reading your autobiography will never know that."

The sound of E.C. tired laughter as I closed the door behind me

17

made me smile, but with the other writer quitting during the tour, the publishing schedule for this project was tight. The last autobiography I worked on took me a full eighteen months to research and write. I had just ten months to finish this one in time for Crossfire's next tour. It was going to be a challenge.

CHAPTER 2

I walked toward my apartment, eagerly anticipating getting out of my wrinkled traveling clothes, putting on my favorite soft PJ's and organizing my notes. The happy, busy hum of Manhattan was in my ears when my phone buzzed. The number was unfamiliar, but I knew better than to ignore it. My mom has a habit of losing her phone and borrowing from strangers. I never know when it might be her.

"Hello?" I answered.

Silence.

"Mom? Is that you?"

"Hello?" The voice was older, unfamiliar, with an accent I couldn't place. "You are Amy Stanton? Yes?"

"I'm Amy." I ducked into a coffee shop to escape the noise. "Who is this?"

"I am Erma Yoder. Rick Downey's neighbor."

Rick Downey! I hadn't heard that name in ages. My pulse sped up. "Is everything okay?"

"No," Erma's voice trembled. "It is not okay."

"What's wrong?" I gripped the phone tighter.

"We called the ambulance, but... they couldn't save him."

Her words landed like a physical blow. My knees went weak, and I sank into the nearest chair. The noise of the city outside faded.

Rick? Gone?

My mind struggled to process Erma's words while life continued to swirl around me. People placed orders, cups and saucers clinked, the espresso machine hissed.

"He told me, if anything happened, to make sure you knew," Erma said. "He kept your number by the phone," Erma said.

Rick had my cell phone number. I didn't know that.

"Thank you for calling me. I don't... I don't know what to say."

"You do not need to say anything," Erma sounded caring and understanding. "Words are not important now. But... will you make the funeral arrangements? Rick never talked about having any other family. Only you, his daughter."

Whoa! What?

"Stepdaughter," I explained. "I was his stepdaughter. I'm not really related to him. Rick was my mother's third husband."

"Oh," Erma absorbed that. "He never explained it to me. He was just always so proud of you and your writing."

My throat tightened. Rick had followed my career? He had spoken about me like I was his daughter. Why hadn't I known this? Why hadn't he contacted me earlier if that was how he felt?

"I will plan the funeral, then," Erma said after a pause. "Lucas will help."

"Who is Lucas?" I asked, my mind spinning.

"He is Rick's farm manager," Erma explained. "A good boy, that one!"

Rick owned a farm. That was unexpected. When he was with my mother, he had been a sophisticated art appraiser for Sotheby's in New York City. The idea of Rick owning a farm seemed wildly uncharacteristic.

"Will you come to the funeral?" Erma's question pulled me back to the present.

"Yes, of course," I replied automatically. "Where exactly are you?"

"I am calling from Rick's house in Sugarcreek."

"Sugarcreek?"

"It is in Ohio," she said, as if that should be obvious. "The tourists call this area Amish Country."

Amish Country. That explained her accent.

"Please call me when you know the details," I said. "And thank you for getting in touch."

I disconnected the call and sat still, trying to process everything I had just learned. A deep sense of hurt settled into my chest. Rick might not have been my blood relative, but he had been a father to me when I needed one the most. Rick was the only real dad I had ever known. Desiree had destroyed all that.

The warmth of the coffee shop enveloped me, but inside I felt cold. Sadness, regret, and guilt hit me all at once. I had let so many years slip by without reaching out. How could I have let that happen?

My thoughts drifted to my mother. She would need to know, of course, but I hesitated to call, even though I still clutched the phone in my hand. The memory of the last time I had seen Rick—during the ugly divorce that my mother had forced on him—came flooding back. He'd looked so hurt, but Mom had made me turn my back on him.

At twelve, I'd had no choice. She was my mother. In the years that followed, she never once mentioned Rick's name or allowed me to. She had always acted as though Rick ceased to exist the moment the ink dried on the divorce papers. For me, it had been quite different. I missed him terribly, but Desiree never budged on allowing him visitation.

On my eighteenth birthday, I had hoped Rick would get in touch. When he didn't, I figured he had forgotten all about me. I imagined him remarried to someone nicer than my mom, with a couple of lucky biological children of his own. I even wondered if he was angry with me for not fighting harder to be part of his life during their divorce. As an adult, I never tried to reach out to him.

I wondered if my mother would even care about this news. It was possible that she would receive it with complete indifference. I shoved my phone back into my pocket. I would deal with Desiree later. Right now, I needed to process this on my own. Rick was gone, and with him, a special six years of my childhood I had not realized I still clung to.

I would go to Ohio. I would attend the funeral. And somehow, I would find a way to make peace with everything I had not said, everything I had not done during these past ten years when despite my mother's disapproval, I could have had a relationship with the most caring father a child could have ever asked for.

CHAPTER 3

Two days after Erma's phone call, I drove through the Ohio countryside searching for the Walnut Creek Mennonite church. The Sugarcreek, Ohio, area was beautiful. It looked like something straight out of an airbrushed travel brochure. The early morning mist gave everything an other-worldly feel as I tried to avoid bumping into one of the dozens of black buggies ahead of me as we all crawled toward the Walnut Creek Mennonite Church. The rent-a-car company at the airport had upgraded me to a giant SUV, which was not the easiest vehicle to drive on the winding, narrow roads. Especially since I rarely touched the wheel of a car. Uber and the NYC trains and subway system were my friends.

I expected a small gathering, a handful of people who had known Rick. Instead, every Amish person in the country seemed to be turning out for his funeral. I allowed myself a glance in the rearview mirror, then slammed on the brakes as the buggy in front of me stopped abruptly. My recorder, purse, and the remnants of a McDonald's mocha went flying.

"Calamity Jane strikes again," I muttered, echoing my mother's familiar comment every time I did something clumsy. My mother wouldn't be here today, which wasn't a surprise. Desireé Stanton didn't do funerals. She didn't do weddings, either, unless they were her own.

The church building was large and modern, and the parking lot was spacious. After parking, I mopped up the mocha as best I could with napkins, gathered my scattered belongings, and walked into the church, feeling like an outsider in a world I did not understand.

About three hundred voices were singing an unfamiliar hymn. There was no pipe organ, and I had never heard a hymn sung with such unified voices. A middle-aged Amish woman near the back scooted over and gestured toward the space, and I gratefully sank onto the pew. As the hymns swirled around me, I let memories of Rick flood my thoughts.

Rick had stepped into my life when I was only six. He lifted me up into his arms as though delighted to have a little daughter, even one who was already dragging emotional baggage behind her like a tattered suitcase. Desireé had often been too wrapped up in her career to notice her only child's needs, but Rick somehow made me feel like I was a treasured gift instead of a nuisance.

When the microphone got passed around so people could share their memories, I reached for it. I seldom choose to speak in public if I didn't have to, but I knew I'd never forgive myself if I didn't say *something*.

"Rick Downey was my stepfather when I was a child," I began, my voice shaking with emotion. "He cut the crusts off my sandwiches and sewed up the rips in my blue velvet bunny when my mom's poodle puppy got hold of it. He was the most decent, caring person I've ever known."

There were many more words I could have said, but they caught in my throat, and I choked into silence. I handed the mic to the next person and sank back down onto the pew as others shared their own memories of the small kindnesses of my favorite ex-stepfather.

After the service, I lingered in the aisle, surrounded by people chatting. I was unsure of where to go or what to do.

A middle-aged Amish woman with a kind face approached me, her hand outstretched. "I'm Erma. I'm glad you got here safely. Will you be going to the cemetery with us?"

The cemetery. I'd forgotten about that part. I was not well-versed in funeral culture. This was only the second one I'd ever been to—a college classmate I had not known well. There had been no cemetery involved with that one. Only an urn with ashes and lots of photos.

My worry must have shown.

"You must be tired from the trip. If you want to skip the gravesite and go straight to the house, I have it all ready for you."

"House?" I asked, confused.

"Rick's, of course," she replied, surprised. "He'd want you to stay there."

The invitation brought fresh tears to my eyes. I tried to hold them back, but they spilled over. I dabbed at them with a balled-up tissue from my purse.

"Here, child," an elderly woman in a gauzy white bonnet offered me a clean cloth hanky with lace around the edges. "Those paper tissues just don't hold up at a funeral. Use this. Don't bother giving it back. I have plenty."

I took the hanky, mumbling my thanks as I tried to compose myself. By now, a small group of women, mostly Amish, had gathered around me, their presence both comforting and overwhelming.

"So, this is Rick's daughter?" one of them whispered.

"I guess so," another replied.

"The ghost writer?"

"Yes, the one from New York City."

"Oh, the poor little thing!" The pity in their voices made me feel even worse. I wasn't sure if they felt sorry for my loss of Rick or because I lived in New York City.

"She writes about ghosts?"

"I don't know. Maybe."

"I left supper on the stove," Erma said gently, cutting through the murmurs. "And there's chocolate cake in the refrigerator. The house is all clean and ready. You'll be comfortable there after your long trip."

"I... I reserved a room at The Victorian Inn," I stammered, still reeling from everything that had happened.

"My cousin owns that," Erma replied with a smile. "I'll call and let her know you won't be coming. She'll understand."

"Do you think his daughter will stay for the funeral dinner?" one of the women whispered.

"I don't know. She probably should. "

"She looks so tired."

I felt a rising panic, a desperate need to escape the well-meaning scrutiny of these women. I teetered on the edge of running straight out the door.

Erma handed me a piece of notebook paper with a map drawn on it in pencil. "You should have no trouble finding it. The key is under the porch mat. Fresh milk is in the refrigerator. Lucas always drops off a quart in Rick's refrigerator after morning milking, plus a pound of butter once a week. If you like eggs for breakfast, there's a henhouse out back. Oh, and Lucas always makes sure there's plenty of firewood in case it gets nippy."

Her words blurred together—eggs, milk, butter, firewood, Lucas. I clutched the map, nodding numbly. Given all options, going to Rick's house seemed the easiest way out.

"In fact, there's Lucas right now," she gestured toward a tall Amish man standing by the church door, talking with several others. He wore black pants with a white shirt and a black coat, just like every other bearded Amish man in the place. His gaze was direct and somber as he saw us looking at him.

"He's the one who found Rick," she added softly.

I took a deep breath and approached him, unsure of what to say.

But before I could open my mouth, the farm manager disappeared out the door.

"That's odd," Erma mused. "He's normally so friendly. Oh well. You'll meet him soon enough."

CHAPTER 4

Hearing the clip-clop of his horse's hooves on the packed dirt road usually brought Lucas comfort. It was a rhythm that matched the steady pace of his life. Not today, however. The thing troubling him today was figuring out what would happen to Rick's farm. Who would inherit the place? If he knew—he could figure out what to do.

Rick had no blood kin that Lucas knew about. No one with a solid claim to the land that Lucas had poured his soul into. Lucas didn't even know if Rick had a will. If he did, he might have left it to that city girl—Rick's stepdaughter, who had never come to visit. The one whose childhood photo was on Rick's refrigerator.

The realization gnawed at him, stirring a mixture of anger and sorrow. He knew it wasn't fair to judge her before they had exchanged a single word, but she didn't look like someone who would want to belong in this farming community. Lucas doubted she had ever walked barefoot through a freshly plowed field or experienced dirt beneath her fingernails from planting seeds that would one day grow into food for the table. What could this farm mean to someone like her?

The answer was obvious. The farm would mean nothing to her. It was just another piece of property, an inheritance potentially to be sold off to the highest bidder. He could see it clearly unfolding in his mind—the barns emptied, the fields sold, the land divided up for new housing developments. It made his stomach hurt. It was happening all around.

As his horse trotted on, Lucas considered his options. He could stay at his brother's place for a while until he found another farm to rent. It wasn't an ideal solution, but it was practical. The problem was that the window for getting crops in the ground for this year was closing fast.

There was also the matter of his livestock. The cattle were his, not Rick's, and he couldn't just leave them behind. He would need time to sell them or find a place where they could be moved. He hoped this stepdaughter of Rick's would be lenient enough to give him time to do that.

It wouldn't be hard for her to find a buyer if she wanted to sell. The Tuscarawas-Holmes County area was considered idyllic by many, a perfect slice of Amish countryside that people from the city dreamed of owning. And in this, at least, Lucas had to agree with them. It was a special place, and one worth preserving.

One thing was for certain: he would not wait around long.

Rick had loaned him a book by C.S. Lewis, a famous Christian writer. In the book, Lewis had referred to the "laziness of grief." It had resonated with Lucas, because he knew firsthand that grief dragged a lot of other emotions along with it. He'd experienced the peculiar sort of inertia that caused a hard-working man to become unable to do anything except exist after experiencing a great loss.

It was Rick who had sought him out and given him a job, a home, and the time to pull himself together after he lost his sweet wife. He was going to miss Rick, but he would not allow himself to experience that inertia again. He couldn't afford to.

Unless, perhaps, Rick had left the farm to him.

No.

He shoved the thought out of his mind. He refused to even allow himself to think about it. Rick had already given him enough.

CHAPTER 5

"Are you Amy Stanton?" A young woman, clearly not Amish, introduced herself to me as I was trying to escape. Her sharp, tailored outfit and the confident way she carried herself made her stand out among the simpler dresses and bonnets. She looked more like someone who came from New York City than I did.

I had hoped to slip away from the church unnoticed. There had been about as much social interaction for one day as I could handle. But getting away turned out to be harder than I expected.

"Yes," I said. "I'm Amy."

"I'm Cassie Reynolds." Her tone was professional. "I'm Rick Downey's attorney."

"Okay." I replied, wondering what this had to do with me.

The other women drifted away, their whispers fading as they gave us space. Cassie gestured toward a door off to the side of the auditorium. "I know this isn't the best time, but there are a few things I need to ask you. Pastor Thomas has allowed us to use his office for privacy. It won't take long."

I hesitated; not sure I was ready to deal with whatever she wanted to talk about. Perhaps she thought I knew things about Rick's family connections. I didn't. He'd mentioned no relatives to me I could remember. Still, I intended to leave tomorrow morning, so if there was something she truly needed to know, it needed to be dealt with now. I doubted I'd ever come back here.

I followed her into the small, wood-paneled room.

Cassie closed the door behind us and motioned for me to sit in a chair near the desk. The room smelled faintly of old books. I sat down and clasped my hands together as Cassie sat opposite me and opened a black leather tote. Within it was a sheaf of papers she pulled out.

"I'm sorry to have to do this now," Cassie said. "But Rick wanted you to be informed as soon as possible. He left explicit instructions."

"Instructions?"

Cassie handed me a document. "This is a copy of his will. He named you his primary beneficiary."

I stared at the paper in my hands, trying to process what she had just said. "His... beneficiary?" I repeated,

Cassie nodded. "It's a very simple will. Rick left everything to you. The farm, the house, his business. It's all yours."

I felt the blood drain from my face. "But... why? I haven't seen him in years."

"Rick was proud of the woman you've become," Cassie said. "He wanted you to know that."

I blinked back tears.

"I... I don't know what to say," I stammered, staring down at the will, the words swimming before my eyes. "I know nothing about running a farm, or Rick's business... and I have a book to write."

"You don't have to decide anything right now," Cassie reassured me. "The farm isn't going anywhere, and neither am I. I'll be here to help with whatever you need. I'm sure Lucas will help, too."

I nodded, my mind a whirlwind. "I need time to think," I murmured, more to myself than to her. "I've never even seen the place."

"Of course," Cassie replied, standing at the same time as I rose to my feet. "This is a lot to take in. Here's my card. Call me when you're ready to talk."

I took the card, tucking it into my purse, still grasping the will in my hand. The room felt stifling as I fumbled my way to the door. Cassie opened it for me.

"I'll be in touch," she said as I stepped back into the church, the murmurs of the remaining mourners a distant hum in my ears.

I barely registered the people around me as I made my way back to my car. I had come here to say goodbye, not to inherit Rick's life—a life I did not know how to live.

By the time I reached the SUV, I was shaking. I climbed in and gripped the steering wheel. My life felt like it had suddenly spiraled completely out of my control.

CHAPTER 6

Rick's house was only a few miles away, but it felt like a journey into another world. The road wound through fields and pastures, the landscape a patchwork of soft greens and fruit trees covered in buds about to bloom. It was beautiful, in a way that made my heart ache. I could see why Rick had settled here, why he had chosen this life. The beauty of it felt healing.

When I arrived, my breath caught in my throat. Rick's white, two-story house, with its dark green roof and enormous porch, stood at the end of a long, curved driveway. Black and white cattle grazed on the hillside behind it.

A smaller house, exactly matching Rick's, sat slightly behind the larger one. The gravel driveway continued past the two houses to a massive red barn. A black buggy sat directly outside. A glossy brown horse frisked inside a fenced-in pasture beside it. In the distance, I could see a nearly endless vista of rolling hills with trees dressed in their gentle spring foliage. The sun hung low, casting a golden glow over everything.

The place was stunning.

I parked, climbed out of the car, and the quiet hit me. The solid-looking farmhouse with its wide wrap-around porch seemed to welcome me. After the emotions of the funeral and the meeting with Cassie, it was all a bit much.

I found the key under the second mat I tried—the one at the back of the house—and stepped into the kitchen. The scent of freshly baked bread surprised me, but there it was—a perfect homemade loaf.

I lifted the lid of a small blue pot on the stove and breathed in the rich aroma of chicken and noodles—Erma's promised supper. A note from her lay on the table.

Come see me if you need anything. I'm your nearest neighbor to the north. Lucas Hershberger lives in the little Daadi Haus behind you. He will also be happy to help in any way he can.

I spotted an old refrigerator, the kind with rounded corners, in the corner. My breath caught again when I saw what was on its door—a yellowing photo of me, a first grader with pigtails, a big smile, and a missing front tooth.

That day came rushing back. My loose tooth had fallen out that morning, my hair wouldn't behave, and my favorite sweater had lost a button. Rick had tamed my hair, sewn on the button, and convinced me to smile despite the gap in my teeth.

Mom had slept through it all.

Seeing that picture now broke the final dam within me. Rick had loved me so much he had kept a childhood photo of me on his fridge. My heart ached with emotions I didn't even know how to name.

I collapsed into a kitchen chair, laid my head on the table, and sobbed.

Lucas watched quietly from the barn as Rick's daughter pulled in. Should he go welcome her to Rick's farm? Give her his condolences? Offer coffee? Hand her his resignation?

He wasn't really in the mood, but like most Amish, he had been taught to do the right thing regardless of how he felt, so he headed to the house to pay his respects.

He had spoken with *Englisch* women over the years, of course, but rarely and seldom easily. It sometimes felt like he was trying to communicate with a different species, especially when they stood there in front of him in immodest clothing, heavy makeup, and jangly jewelry. It made him feel tongue-tied and weary just thinking about it.

Rehearsing what to say to her, he stepped onto the back porch. His hand was poised to knock when he heard sobs from the other side of the door in the kitchen.

The woman was crying her heart out. The raw sound of it shocked him. Perhaps he had judged her too harshly. If he were Rick, he would go in and try to comfort her. But he was not Rick. He was just himself, an Amish farmer who was clumsy with words. He decided he would speak to her tomorrow after the crying stopped. Careful to make no sound, he went back to his *Daadi Haus*.

CHAPTER 7

After I cried myself out, I wandered through Rick's house, sniffling, trying to decide where to sleep. The place was spacious, uncluttered, and decorated with various quilts and framed photos of the Amish countryside. The walls were painted in soft pastel colors, and the furniture was solid, handcrafted oak. Being inside Rick's house felt like a hug, even though my entire apartment could fit into the main bedroom alone.

Once I'd familiarized myself with the layout of the house, I reheated the chicken and noodles Erma had left for me, cut a slice of her homemade bread, and spread a thick layer of butter on it. The chocolate cake called out to me, but I decided to save that indulgence for later.

I took my supper out to the back porch, settling into a porch swing while watching the sun dip below the horizon. The quiet was a far cry from the constant noise and bustle of New York City. Even though I was used to city noises, I felt the muscles in my neck and shoulders relax for the first time in months. I took a deep breath and savored the scent of spring in the air.

I stayed out there until it grew dark and chilly. Then I washed my dishes and put the kitchen in order. I slept on the couch instead of disturbing any of the bedrooms. After all, I was only here for one night, and even though the house was technically mine now, I couldn't shake the feeling of being a trespasser. I spent most of the night tossing and turning. Not because the couch wasn't comfortable—it was—but because I was trying to wrap my mind around the ramifications of what had happened today.

Inheriting this place meant I now owned a beautiful home with no rent, no worrisome bank loan, and no troubling homeowner association fees. I did not deserve such a gift, and I certainly hadn't earned it, but wow. My heart felt close to bursting with gratitude.

Living in Manhattan was expensive, and because it was so expensive, I was barely scraping by. My mom was rich, I suppose—she didn't choose to share her financial information with me—but that did not mean that I was. I'd gotten through college on scholarships, loans, and working as a nanny during the summers. Mom hadn't offered to help, and I had not asked.

Moving here would mean living life without worrying over how soon the next writing check might appear. Moving here would also mean giving up my life in New York City, with my friends, my favorite coffee shop, and proximity to my publisher, agent, and editor. It was familiar, it was what I knew, and I tended to cling to familiarity. I think it was because I'd had enough adventure while following my mom around in those early years to last a lifetime.

Boring was good. I could embrace a normal, unexciting life with enthusiasm.

Finally, giving up on sleep, I left the couch and headed to the refrigerator, where the chocolate cake waited. I poured a glass of cold milk from the glass jar, grabbed a fork, and dug in.

A half hour later, sufficiently loaded up on sugar and chocolate, I made that phone call to my mom. It was late, but I seldom knew what time zone she was in, and right now I didn't much care. I needed information, and I needed it now if I was ever going to get any rest.

CHAPTER 8

"Hi Mom," I said. "You got a minute?"

"Hello, darling!" She sounded carefree. There was jazz music playing in the background and voices. "Of course I have time! How are you?"

"I'm not sure."

"What?" I heard her say a few muffled words to someone. When she answered again, the background noise was muted. Apparently, she'd found a slightly quieter spot. "Now say that again, but make it quick. We're going to a different party soon."

"Where are you?" I couldn't help myself.

"New Orleans," she said. "I told you about that film I was producing."

She hadn't. But producing? That was new.

"We just wrapped everything up and we're having a little celebration. Why are you calling me so late?" she said. "It must be all of midnight in New York. You usually go to bed with the chickens."

I heard her chuckle at her little joke, and I caught the accidental irony. She didn't know how close to the truth she was tonight.

"I'm not in New York, Mom. I'm in Ohio. Rick's funeral was earlier today. Remember? I told you about it."

"I'm sorry, sweetie. I forgot." She sounded distracted. "Are you okay?"

"No, Mom. I'm not okay."

Silence. I knew she was calculating whether to talk to me about Rick or make an excuse and get back to her celebration.

I waited. Counting beats while she wavered. Then I heard a sigh. She'd chosen to be a mother for a few minutes instead of a party girl. I heard her high heels clicking as she walked further away from the noise. Finally, there was silence.

"Okay. I can talk now." Her voice lost its festive quality and morphed into what I knew as normal. "What's happened? Why are you still in Ohio? Don't you have a deadline? I thought you'd be back in New York by now."

"Nope. I decided to stay at Rick's house."

"Why?"

"Well, for one thing, it belongs to me now."

"Wait. What? Rick made you his heir?"

"According to his lawyer, he did."

The silence went on and on. I hoped she would respond with understanding. I hoped I could talk to her about the mixed emotions I was feeling. I hoped she wouldn't…

But she did.

"That's wonderful, Amy!" Desiree purred. "How much was Rick worth?"

The conversation after that wasn't what I'd hoped for.

"I don't know yet, Mom. That's not why I called. What I want is for you to tell me what happened when I was twelve. Why didn't you ever allow me to see him again? Taped to his refrigerator is a school picture of me when I was six. Didn't he at least try to get visitation?"

"He tried," Mom said. "But I shot that down."

"Why? How?"

"I threatened to spread rumors about him if he fought me on it."

"Rumors?"

"You know what I mean. I could have said anything I wanted to about him, accused him publicly of all sorts of things, and people would have believed me."

"But he was never anything but good to me, and he was good to you, too!"

"I know that, but good men can be boring, sweetheart."

"Not when you are twelve and he's the only real father you've ever known!" My anger shocked even me.

"I was seeing Franco by then and I didn't want Rick coming around all the time to visit you. It would have felt creepy."

"I cried myself to sleep for weeks. Months."

"It couldn't be helped. Franco didn't like Rick and didn't want him around after we got married, and face it, darling, you recovered."

"No, Mom, I didn't."

"Well, it's all water under the bridge now, anyway." She changed the subject. "Tell me about Rick's house. Is it nice? I'm free for a few days after we finish filming next week. I can come for a visit, and we can decide what to do with it."

My insides felt like they were boiling. It seemed a good idea to disconnect before I said things we might never recover from, and so I did. She didn't call back.

CHAPTER 9

E arly the next morning, I dragged myself off the couch and wandered over to the kitchen window, grateful I'd scheduled a one o'clock flight back to New York and didn't have to rush this morning.

An enormous red wooden barn, a fenced-in chicken yard, and acres upon acres of pasture dotted with black and white cattle greeted me. So. Many. Cows.

Overnight, I had become the bleary-eyed owner of Old MacDonald's farm! What, exactly, was one supposed to do with that many cows?

I sighed and whispered, "What were you thinking, Rick?"

Fluffy golden hens were scratching and pecking inside the large chicken pen. They looked adorable, like something you'd want to cuddle. I wondered if they enjoyed being petted. I'd never owned a pet, but I liked the thought of it.

A real country woman would probably already be out there, gathering eggs while humming a cheerful song, like something straight out of Little House on the Prairie, which had been my favorite program when I was young. I could almost see Laura Ingalls skipping around with her basket, making it look easy and fun.

I decided I could probably gather eggs without first being shown how. It shouldn't be more difficult than hunting Easter eggs, and I'd loved doing that as a child. There was even an old-fashioned egg basket hanging from a hook on the screened-in back porch.

So, without bothering to change out of my black silk pajamas and matching robe—a Christmas gift from my mother, who had been appalled at my cotton flannel pajamas on one visit—I decided to dip my toes into the proverbial waters of farm life. I slipped my feet into my shoes, went out the back door onto the porch, grabbed the egg basket, and walked out to the chicken pen, feeling pleased with myself.

Look at me, a farm girl! Getting ready to gather eggs from my very own chickens in my very own chicken coop! It was absurdly satisfying. I could hardly wait to tell my friends back in the city all about what I'd done.

That blissful feeling lasted right up until the moment I unlatched the door to the chicken yard and stepped inside. I failed to notice the not-so-adorable rooster strutting around among the hens. Unfortunately, the rooster *had* noticed me! With a wild flap of wings, it flew straight at my face, spurs first.

"Yah!" I screamed, flailing the egg basket at it with one hand, while trying to protect my head and face with the other. The hens scattered in all directions, squawking. The rooster, unimpressed with my pitiful attempts to defend myself, launched another attack. I was dealing with a bird that had one mission in life: to protect those chickens.

The next few moments were a blur of flapping wings, sharp pecks, lots of hens flying around, and sheer panic on my part. The rooster seemed to be everywhere at once, trying to hold its balance on my head and shoulders as it continued its relentless assault. My screams for help echoed through the empty farmyard as I sprinted for the house, the egg basket still flailing wildly.

Just as I reached the safety of the screened-in porch, I managed to fling the evil creature off me, slamming the door behind me and locking it with trembling hands. The rooster, clearly still furious, flew at the screen door twice more before giving up and strutting around outside like some kind of poultry thug. It might as well have been saying, "You want a piece of me? Well, do you? Come on out. I dare you!"

I looked down at my left hand, which was now throbbing from a deep spur-inflicted scratch. Muttering to myself, I hurried into the kitchen sink and held my hand beneath a stream of cold water. I couldn't believe I hadn't realized there might be a rooster in the chicken yard. I might be from the city, but I wasn't that ignorant! I knew roosters didn't exactly welcome strangers with open winged hospitality. But goodness, who knew roosters could be that mean!

So much for skipping around the chicken pen gathering eggs. My good mood had evaporated, replaced by a sudden aversion to eggs. The stupid hens and their stupid rooster could keep their stupid eggs forever, as far as I was concerned. I'd eat toast for breakfast from now on.

CHAPTER 10

L ucas loved early mornings. He usually awoke with a sense of anticipation toward the day ahead, ready to tackle whatever project needed doing on the farm. But today was different. Today, he awoke with a heavy heart, and it took him a few moments to remember why.

Ah, yes. Rick was gone. The loss of his good friend weighed heavily on him, and he missed their daily conversations, their shared work, and the quiet camaraderie that had grown over the years. And then there was the matter of Rick's *Englisch* daughter. Her sudden appearance, along with his uncertainty about what Rick had done about the ownership of the farm, cast a shadow on the day. He dreaded meeting her.

God did not promise an easy life, Lucas reminded himself as he lay there in the predawn stillness. That was one thing you could depend on. But Lucas had prayed long and hard about this situation last night before going to sleep, and he trusted that whatever the Lord decided, he would accept.

With a sigh, he climbed out of bed, pulling on and buttoning his broadfall trousers. Then he reached for a plain gray work shirt and pulled it over his head, the worn cotton fabric familiar and comforting. Hitching homemade suspenders over his shoulders—his sister made his clothing for him now that he no longer had a wife—he made his way to the kitchen, ready to start his day.

Breakfast was a quiet, almost sacred routine for Lucas. He reached for the bowl and the jar of homemade granola—a recipe his late wife had perfected years ago. He'd made dozens of pans of it since she passed, not just because it was easy, but because it filled the kitchen with the warm, sweet smell of her memory. As he spooned the granola into a bowl, he could almost feel her presence, as if she were still there, sharing the quiet morning with him.

Lucas settled at the kitchen table with his breakfast. His gaze drifted to the large window that faced east. The sky was just beginning to blush with the first hints of dawn, the promise of a beautiful sunrise spreading across the horizon. He closed his eyes, giving a short but heartfelt prayer of gratitude. It would be a good day to plow, but the chances were good that he would no longer be here for the harvest.

There were repairs waiting in the barn—old tack that needed mending, minor tasks that kept the place in order. If he had to leave this farm, he wanted to leave it in good repair, just as Rick would have wanted. The thought gave him a sense of purpose, enough to fill his head with a pleasant plan for the day. He was even ready to face the less pleasant tasks, like shoveling manure.

He was deep into that very chore when he heard it—a woman's scream, sharp and panicked, cutting through the morning air. His heart lurched. It had to be Rick's stepdaughter—but what on earth was happening to the woman? Without a second thought, he dropped the shovel and sprinted toward the sound, rounding the edge of the house just in time to witness a sight he would never forget—nor would he ever want to.

There was Amy, clad in long black pajamas, sprinting toward the house with her bathrobe flying behind her. But that wasn't the alarming part. Perched on her head, flapping its wings and pecking furiously, was Zedekiah, the most beautiful rooster Lucas had ever seen. He was also the meanest.

Lucas might have intervened, but he paused, both startled and bemused. Amy was doing a pretty good job of waging her own battle. She managed to swat the rooster away just as she reached the safety of the screened porch, slamming the door behind her and latching it.

Zedekiah strutted back and forth outside the door, puffed up with self-importance, as if daring her to step outside and face him again. That bird had been nothing but trouble from the start, but watching it now, Lucas chuckled at its sheer audacity.

Amy, in her haste, had left the chicken yard door wide open. During the fray, many hens had scattered out into the yard. With a sigh, Lucas walked over to close the pen before more hens made a run for it. Then he turned his attention to Zedekiah, who was still busy showing off his contempt for Amy, even though she'd already gone inside the house.

"Well, Zedekiah," he muttered, "you sure know how to make an impression." The rooster, unimpressed, flapped his wings and crowed, still full of himself.

CHAPTER 11

Once I rinsed my hand off at the sink, I wrapped it in a clean dish towel and stood in the kitchen, trying to decide if the cut on my hand required a trip to urgent care for stitches. Then I wondered if there was even an urgent care place near here. I was still pondering that when I heard a loud squawk outside, followed by a frantic flapping of wings, and then…silence.

What in the world was happening now?

A moment later, I heard a quiet knock at the door. I wrapped my hand in a clean dish towel, carefully opened the door, peeked out, and saw Lucas Hershberger standing there, holding a struggling rooster beneath his arm.

My jaw dropped, and I stepped out onto the screened-in porch. "Is that the rooster that attacked me?"

"It is," he replied calmly, as if holding a struggling, enraged bird was the most natural thing in the world. "Do you want me to kill him for you?"

He said it so matter-of-factly that I wondered if I'd misheard him. "Kill it? Why would you do that?"

"Because you said to."

"I did no such thing."

"You did. You were running and screaming. These are your exact words…" He cleared his throat. "Holy crap! Somebody get this demon bird off me! Kill it! Kill it!"

I blinked in surprise. "I said all that?"

Lucas confirmed with a slight nod. "And a few other words I do not wish to repeat."

I felt my face flush with embarrassment. "I apologize for my language, but that thing is vicious."

"And you are *Englisch*," he said, as if that explained everything.

It took me a moment to realize that he was implying my outburst was simply something to be expected from someone who wasn't Amish. I wasn't sure whether to be offended or amused by his calm acceptance of my outburst.

He held the rooster out toward me. It was a deep, reddish black, so young and healthy its feathers glistened in the sun. Now that it was not trying to kill me, I could appreciate the beauty of it. "Do you want it?"

I took a step back, horrified. "What would I do with it?"

"Cook it," he said, with a hint of amusement. "He's still young enough to be tender and tasty."

"No, no, thank you!" I stammered, shaking my head emphatically.

"You are sure about that?" Lucas's eyes sparkled with a quiet humor. "Zedekiah here would make a fine meal."

It took me a moment to catch on to the fact that he was teasing. That surprised me. I didn't think Amish people teased, especially not solemn-looking men wearing suspenders and beards. But there he was, quietly poking fun at me.

Lucas chuckled softly, then walked over to the chicken yard and set the rooster free inside. I watched it scuttle off; its dignity thoroughly compromised.

"I clipped its spurs," Lucas said. "It will still fly at you, but it won't do as much damage next time."

"There won't be a next time. I can live a long and happy life without ever going near those chickens again. You're Lucas, right?"

"Yes. I am Lucas Hershberger."

"I'm Amy Stanton. Rick's... daughter." I had grown weary of having to explain the relationship. Calling myself his daughter seemed the easiest and simplest thing to do.

Lucas's head cocked to one side. He looked unconvinced.

"I mean, I'm his stepdaughter. Ex-stepdaughter, as a matter of fact. He and my mother divorced when I was twelve. I haven't quite figured out what to say to people when they assume Rick was my father."

Lucas thought this over. "Those of us who heard Rick speak of you do not need to see a birth certificate to know that you were the daughter of his heart."

A bittersweet warmth spread through me at his words. "Thank you for saying that."

With the rooster crisis averted for the moment, I finally took a proper look at Lucas. Beneath the beard, the plain clothes, and the awkward bowl haircut, Rick's farm manager was a striking man. His blue eyes were sharp and clear, and he was tall with broad shoulders that suggested a lifetime of hard work. Even though he didn't appear to be more than mid-thirties, his dark brown hair already had a few silver strands in it. I had a feeling that this rugged-looking man couldn't care less about a few gray hairs.

But then I noticed something else about him. A distinct odor was wafting toward me, sharp and unmistakable.

"If you're wondering what stinks, it's me," Lucas said, as if reading my thoughts. He nodded toward the barn. "I was shoveling horse manure when I heard you scream."

"Thanks for clearing that up for me." I smiled at his bluntness. "I was wondering."

Lucas turned away, but then paused. "You should check those cuts in your hair. I'm afraid Zedekiah got in some good whacks."

"My hair?" I echoed. My right hand flew unbidden to the top of my head and came away bloody. My knees went slack, and I felt a little woozy. Blood and I had never gotten along. As a little girl, I had skipped the I-want-to-be-a-nurse-when-I-grow-up stage. It was one of the nice things about my job as a writer. Compared to most people, I lived a very bloodless life, and I was okay with that.

I hurried to the bathroom, dreading what I'd see in the mirror. The moment I caught sight of my reflection, I recoiled in horror. My hair was a wild mess from the rooster's attack. It stuck out in every direction. A rivulet of blood trickled down my cheek.

There was a knock at the bathroom door. Lucas stuck his head in. "You'd better let me look at those cuts. I have medicine that will help it keep from getting infected."

So, there I was, a few minutes later, sitting on a kitchen chair in my pajamas while Rick's farm manager pawed through my hair, searching for head wounds and applying pressure to the couple he found.

"How is it?" I asked.

"I believe you might live," Lucas said.

Again, with the jokes! "What I meant is, do I need stitches?"

"If you want them. I'm certain the hospital would be happy to shave portions of your scalp to give you a stitch or two."

Oh! I hadn't thought of that. No stitches for me, then. Did they make tiny band aids for peck wounds?

"The bleeding has stopped now, so that is good," he said.

"You said you had medicine?" I wondered if it was some sort of weird homemade Amish thing. "What is it?"

"Triple antibiotic ointment." He pulled a tube out of his back pocket and handed it to me. "If I were you, I'd wash my hair before applying it, but that's your choice."

So, that's exactly what I did. He went back to his chores while I took a quick shower with lots of shampoo, trying not to say "ouch" each time the pecked places stung.

CHAPTER 12

I had showered and was in the downstairs bathroom, wearing my favorite traveling outfit of black, stretchy yoga pants with deep pockets, along with my vintage Purple Rain t-shirt, as I carefully applied the triple antibiotic ointment to the cuts Zedekiah had left on my hand and scalp. The sound of a car door slamming startled me.

I walked into the living room where I could see out the front windows, and I nearly dropped the tube. There, standing beside a taxi, was my mother.

Very little surprised me when it came to Desiree, but hiring a taxi for the hour's drive from the airport was new. She must have been booking plane reservations and traveling ever since we hung up last night, and yet Desireé looked every inch the movie star as she stood outside the taxi in the middle of Ohio farmland.

She wore navy slacks, a white flowy top, and a long, pastel silk scarf around her neck. Her hair was perfectly curled and dyed with a new shade of honey-blonde that shimmered in the sunlight. A hat, sunglasses, and an oversized purse that I'm pretty certain had cost more than a year's worth of my utility bills, completed her ensemble.

However, even without all the trappings of stardom, she was a stunningly beautiful woman. Men fell in love with her at first sight and she used it. The poor taxi driver was probably already composing a sonnet about her.

I walked out onto the front porch in my bare feet and waited.

"Amy! My sweet, sweet girl!" Her voice rang out as she ran up onto the porch and swept me into her arms. I breathed in her lovely scent. She always smelled of whatever expensive hair products her hair stylist was presently using.

"Hello, Mother."

"It is so good to see you!" she gushed. "After that awful phone call, I knew I needed to get here just as soon as I could. I can't bear to have bad feelings between us."

"Can I help you with your luggage?" I asked, already predicting her answer in my mind. She hadn't come to make amends and spend some time together. Desiree was here to see my inheritance, plain and simple.

"Oh, I'm not staying," Desireé replied with a wave of her hand, as if the very idea of staying was absurd. "I just wanted to come see you. I know losing Rick was a terrible blow."

"At twelve, it was a terrible blow," I said. "At thirty, surprisingly, it still is."

She ignored my comment, her eyes already scanning the house. "The place is a little dated, but not bad! Do you like it?"

"Very much."

"I'm scheduled to film in Europe starting next week," she said, eyes darting around as though assessing the house's potential for resale.

"Anything interesting?" I asked politely.

"Not really." Desiree made a face. "Hollywood is not kind to women over forty, Amy. You're so lucky your career doesn't require you to be young and beautiful. Now, show me the house. I need to get back to the airport."

With the taxi waiting, this visit was going to have to be quick. That was fine with me. I led her through the house, trying not to let her comments get under my skin.

She strolled around with her mouth screwed up like a picky eater at a buffet, pointing out flaws I hadn't yet noticed.

"How much acreage did you say comes with the house?" She paused when we arrived back in the living room.

"Two hundred." I sighed, knowing full well where she was going with this.

"Impressive. How much do you think the whole thing is worth?"

"I have no idea." I felt a familiar tension headache building. "I only got here yesterday."

My cell phone buzzed. The number was unfamiliar, so I ignored it.

"You aren't thinking of living here, are you?" She shot me a sharp glance.

"I don't know. I might." I braced myself, fully expecting the thunderstorm of objections that would follow. "I'm still trying to wrap my mind around the fact that it's mine."

Instead of thunder and lightning, I got something worse. Laughter and pity.

"Poor little Amy." She chuckled, then cupped my chin in her hand and looked deep into my eyes. "It's all those Little House on the Prairie episodes you watched with Rick when you were little, isn't it? You wanted to be Laura. You still do."

She wasn't entirely wrong. As a child, I'd wanted to wear long dresses, have pets and siblings, sit around a supper table with my family, and run through a meadow of wildflowers like Laura Ingalls. And honestly, some small part of me still did.

"It would be a nice place to write," I said defensively, feeling a little ridiculous. "It's very peaceful here."

"Farm life is a pretty fantasy when you haven't lived it," Desiree said, "But the reality is a sunburned face, dirt so embedded under your fingernails you can't scrub it out, and a back that aches from shoveling manure all day." Her eyes blazed. "Trust me on this."

"Where is this coming from, Mom?" I took a step back and her hand dropped away from my chin. I'd never heard her talk like this. It wasn't just the words. For a few seconds, her voice had grown rough, and there was a twang to her speech she had meticulously scrubbed out years ago.

Before she could respond, there was a knock on the door. I opened it to find Lucas standing on the porch. "Eggs," he said, handing me the basket I'd used earlier to fend off the rooster.

His face was ruddy from working outdoors, and he looked robust and masculine in a way that made my mother go on red alert. I saw her body language change.

"And who is this?" Her voice dripped with interest. I introduced her to Lucas, who stood silent and stalwart, while she fawned over him in a way that usually had men eating out of her hand.

Lucas barely blinked. His expression was unreadable as she attempted to make light conversation with him.

"Goodbye," he said. And with that, he turned and left. No small talk, no pleasantries. Just Lucas, blunt and straightforward.

My mother was a bit taken aback. "Well, isn't he rustic? I don't think he even realized who I am."

"The man is Amish, Mother." I closed the door behind him. "I don't think they own televisions or watch movies. I can pretty much guarantee he doesn't know who you are."

She looked at me with a mixture of disbelief and curiosity, as though trying to process the idea that someone might exist outside her sphere of fame and influence. For a moment, she seemed lost for words, which was something I had seldom seen happen. I will admit, watching Lucas walking away from her had been very satisfying.

"About the farm, Mom. You sound like you lived on one. I thought you said you'd grown up in L.A."

"The taxi is waiting, sweetheart." Mom was pulling herself together. Scarf, sunglasses, purse. "We'll talk about it another time."

I watched as she climbed into the taxi. We might talk about it another time, or more likely, she'd get a sudden case of amnesia, as she usually did about things she didn't want to address. The only thing I knew about her past before I was born was that she'd been raised in a series of foster homes until she'd aged out of the system. The rest was a mystery and would probably remain one.

CHAPTER 13

Lucas put a potato into the oven to bake and seasoned a steak to fry for his noon meal. His hands still shook slightly at his awkward escape from Amy's mother. He decided he'd rather face a rabid coyote than have another conversation with Desiree Stanton. At least he could shoot a rabid coyote.

Rick Downey had been married to *her*? Seriously? That explained so much. No wonder that quiet, sweet man had been so traumatized he never remarried!

Desiree was just... too much. Too much red lipstick, too much dark eye makeup, too much blonde hair, and too much cleavage. Lucas hadn't known where to look or what to say, and so he left.

Hard to imagine that she had raised Amy. It would be impossible to find two women more different from one another. Amy was quiet, but lovely. Looking into her hazel eyes this morning had been like reading the first paragraphs of a book that you immediately knew you wanted to slow down and savor. Meeting Desiree was like looking at a brightly colored billboard on the side of a road. No depth, just sheer advertisement.

As the scent of frying meat filled his small kitchen, he silently thanked his young wife for insisting that he learn how to cook during their too-short marriage. She had been so insistent, playfully but firmly driving the point home.

"If I die first, you'll need to know how to take care of yourself. I don't want you proposing marriage to the first woman who brings you a casserole!" she'd teased, a twinkle in her eye that made him laugh.

He had wrapped his arms around her, pulling her close as though he could keep her with him forever.

"As if I could ever love anyone else after you," he'd murmured into her hair, breathing in her familiar scent, trying to memorize every detail of her.

But her teasing tone had vanished, replaced by a quiet seriousness that had unsettled him. "If I die first, do not grieve for me too long," she'd said, her voice steady, even though her eyes held a deep sadness. "You are a good man, Lucas. You deserve a good life."

He hadn't understood then. She must have sensed there was something wrong with her. Those words had stuck with him, after they discovered she was ill, echoing in his mind long after she was gone. And while he had learned to cook well enough to fill his stomach, the simple act of preparing a meal did little to dispel the deep loneliness that often crept up on him, especially during these solitary meals.

It would be nice to have someone special to share his life with again, but finding the right Amish woman was only half the battle. The other half was his own uncertainty about his future within the Amish community. He was beginning to doubt he could remain Amish forever. It was getting to be harder and harder with Elmer Yoder as his bishop, and it wouldn't be fair to drag an Amish wife into his spiritual struggles.

Elmer was a good man, yes, but the bishop had a way of single-minded thinking that frustrated Lucas to no end.

For instance, Elmer was not fond of reading—not even the Bible. Unlike many other Amish bishops whom Lucas had known and respected, Elmer seemed to think it was unnecessary to study the Bible when you already knew all the answers. It gnawed at Lucas, especially since he had many questions, and never enough answers.

As he cleaned up after lunch, wiping down the counter and washing the dishes, his thoughts drifted back to the sight of Amy earlier that morning. He could still see her in his mind's eye—those long legs of hers eating up the distance between the henhouse and the back porch, arms flailing, screeching for help as the rooster pursued her with all the ferocity of a barnyard tyrant.

He chuckled to himself. An Amish woman would have handled that situation very differently. Most would have grabbed that rooster by the neck and ended its reign of terror without a second thought. Amish women didn't tolerate such nonsense, and they certainly wouldn't have blundered into an unfamiliar hen yard without keeping an eye out for a rooster. Those spurs could cause real harm if you weren't careful.

Lucas shook his head, still smiling. He decided he'd go back later to see if there was anything else he could do to help Rick's stepdaughter. It was the right thing to do, of course, but he couldn't deny that he was also curious. She was proving to be more entertaining than he'd expected. With no television and little else to distract him except his work, this was a welcome distraction. He found he was not nearly as eager for Amy to leave as he had been at the beginning of the day.

CHAPTER 14

After my mother left, I barely had time to throw my luggage into my rental before a gray SUV rolled up the driveway. Out stepped a tall, skinny man in a dark suit. So much for peace and quiet. Apparently, today was the day my life turned into a revolving door of people.

I stood beside my car and tried to muster up some patience. "Can I help you?"

"Nope. I'm here to help you!" the man said with way too much enthusiasm. He rubbed his hands together, which made him look like some sort of predatory insect. "Name's Stan. I'm a realtor." He shoved a business card into my hand. "Are you Amy Stanton?"

"I am."

"I heard rumors you inherited this place."

My phone buzzed again. Another unfamiliar number, which I ignored. I glanced. "Excuse me, but I really have to go." I opened the door on the driver's side.

He started speaking in a rush. "I've got some people who are very interested in purchasing this place, and I think I can get you an excellent deal if you're ready to sell."

Seriously? The day after Rick's funeral, vultures were already circling. I fought the urge to roll my eyes. "I'm not ready to sell yet," I said. "But I'll keep you in mind if I do. I'm sorry, but I'm late for the airport..."

Stan ignored me. "My clients are highly motivated to buy right now. Not sure they will be if you wait much longer."

"Not a problem." I gave him a look that I hoped conveyed just how little I cared about his motivated clients. "I'm certain there will be others who are interested when, and if, the time comes."

"It's too much property to take care of by yourself," he said, eyeing me like I was about to keel over from the sheer weight of responsibility. "From what I've heard, you're a city girl. I doubt you have the skills needed to keep up with a place this size."

He couldn't have been more infantilizing than if he'd told me not to worry my pretty little head about it. I did not like this man, nor his assumptions.

I opened the driver's side door to my vehicle. "You are right, Stan. I don't know one thing about keeping a place like this running, but that doesn't mean I want to sign papers the day after I buried my stepfather. You do know the funeral was only yesterday, don't you?"

For a moment, he looked taken aback, but quickly recovered. "My condolences." He tried to sound sincere, but his sincerity felt slippery. "But frankly, I don't think you want these buyers to get away."

"Actually, I want them to get away. I want them to get away very much." I opened the car door wider, eager to leave, wanting to be finished with this conversation. "If you'll excuse me..."

Stan wasn't ready to give up, though. "While you're waiting to make up your mind, may I bring them around to check out the place?"

Before I could respond, Lucas appeared from around the side of the house, his expression dark. There was barely restrained anger in his voice when he spoke. "You should be ashamed of yourself!"

"Why?" Stan blinked, all innocence and wide eyes. "What did I do?"

Lucas turned to me. "Stan's 'friends' are trying to find a location for a landfill. They think this valley would be a good fit. Rick had already turned them down twice. Now they're coming after you."

Stan's genial facade evaporated, and a flash of irritation crossed his face. "This isn't your land, Hershberger, and people need someplace to put their trash." He turned back to me, his words dropping into what he probably thought was a reassuring tone. "Trust me, sweetheart, these people are offering a great price. A lot more than the actual property is worth."

A landfill. Here? In this rare and beautiful place? I allowed my inner Desiree to emerge.

"You need to realize something, Stan. I'm not your sweetheart and I've learned to be extremely suspicious of any man who begins a sentence with 'trust me.'"

"But…"

"You need to leave," I said, bluntly.

Stan opened his mouth to argue, but one look at Lucas, who had taken a step closer, and he thought better of it. Without another word, he turned and stalked back to his SUV, slamming the door harder than necessary before he sped off down the driveway.

I let out a long breath I hadn't realized I'd been holding. I glanced around at Rick's property and shook my head. "A landfill? I don't think so!"

Lucas nodded, his gaze lingering on the spot where the SUV had disappeared. "So, Rick did give you the farm?"

"That's what his lawyer told me yesterday. I don't know how this Stan guy found out so soon."

"Lucky guess, probably," he said. "Rick frequently mentioned the little girl he helped raise who had become a bestselling author."

"I don't get it." I slid beneath the steering wheel. "If he cared so much about me, why didn't he ever get in contact after I grew up?"

"I wondered the same thing until this morning."

"What happened this morning?"

"I met your mother!"

71

"She's not that bad." I instantly went on the defensive. She was, after all, my mother. We'd been through a lot together.

"Perhaps not, but Rick knew you were no longer the little girl he'd known. You were becoming a successful writer. He told me he didn't think you'd want anything to do with someone who was just one of your mother's ex-husbands."

"That's not fair!" I burst out in anger and disbelief. "He didn't even give me a chance! I would never have rejected him. I would have loved to have had Rick be part of my life. To learn about all this now that it's too late to talk to him, to tell him how much he meant to me…it hurts!"

I could feel Lucas studying me. "You aren't at all what I imagined."

"And I never imagined you at all because I didn't know that you or this place existed and the closest thing to a father, I ever had was too much of a coward to come find me!"

To his credit, Lucas didn't defend Rick or try to talk me out of my anger and grief.

"I'm sorry," he said. "Rick was wrong."

I started the car and rolled the window down. "Thank you for saying that."

"If it helps, he had a good life here," Lucas said.

"It doesn't," I said. "I wish I could have thanked him for singing me show tunes until I went to sleep each night."

"He sang show tunes for you? Not lullabies?"

"Rick didn't know any lullabies, so he did the best he could. He also chased the monsters out of my closet by banging pots and pans together." I put the car in gear and began to move forward. "Mom hated that."

"I'll pack up the *Daadi Haus* and start looking for different work now that I know for certain he left the farm to you."

I braked. "Why on earth would you do that?"

"Because Rick hired me and you didn't," Lucas said. "This is your place now. It's time I moved on."

I could feel my heart sink. Among everything else Lucas did—whatever it all was—who would feed Zedekiah and his harem of hens if Lucas left? Certainly not me!

"So, here's the thing." I glanced at my watch again. "I want to continue this conversation, but I barely have enough time to make it to the airport in time to get through TSA. Can we just leave things as they are for now? Don't go looking for another job. If Rick hired you, that's good enough for me. I'll come back in a few weeks, and we can sort everything out."

"If you are sure." He stepped away from the car.

"I'm sure. Please do whatever you normally do to take care of the place while I'm gone."

"There are crops that should be planted soon."

"Then, by all means, plant them!"

He looked relieved. "I'll be here."

As I drove away, the knowledge that he would be waiting when I got back was surprisingly comforting.

CHAPTER 15

"Excuse me. So sorry. Oops. Excuse me."
I crawled over two other passengers, fell into my seat, stuffed the black backpack I always carried my laptop in beneath the seat in front of me, and fumbled around to get my seatbelt sorted out. Then I took a deep breath and felt my pulse slow. I'd made it with zero minutes to spare.

Some people get nervous during takeoff. I am not one of them. What with flying back and forth between Los Angeles and New York City for Desiree's various singing and acting gigs, I had more air miles beneath my belt by the time I was ten than most first year commercial pilots.

I tend to fall asleep the minute the plane taxis down the runway. I usually wake up when the refreshment cart rolls around, have a quick snack, then pull out my laptop and go to work. But sometimes I end up sitting beside someone who entertains themselves by reading what I'm writing. That was the case today.

When I'm writing fiction, I don't mind so much, but this is not fiction. It contains details about Ezekiel Cross's life that are not yet ready for the public.

Since I can't force someone with whom I'm sitting shoulder to shoulder to keep their eyes off my glowing laptop page, I shut it down and slipped it back into my backpack.

Forced to go old school, I pulled out a notebook and begin to make notes on the meeting with E.C. My cursive tends to be nearly illegible, so that worked out well. My seatmate fell asleep, and I did my best to shove away all thoughts of Rick, Lucas, and Sugarcreek as I prepared for the meeting.

Three hours later, I caught up with E.C. at the same hotel suite where I had last seen him. It was nice to see that the suite was now fully stocked with cases of bottled spring water and E.C. seemed happy.

"How did the concert go?" I asked.

"It went good!" he said. "But you disappeared on me girl, I tried to get hold of you all morning. Where'd you go?"

I wasn't sure how I felt about being called 'girl' by a client, but I let it slide. He was in a good mood, and I didn't want to mess with that. I plopped down on the couch, feeling more tired than I wanted to admit.

"I was at a funeral in Ohio," I explained. "I've been traveling back to New York most of today."

He sat across from me in an overstuffed chair and crossed his long legs. He was wearing what I think were pajamas today—but it was hard to tell. E.C. wore what he wore.

"Whose funeral?" His tone shifted from slightly annoyed to concerned.

"My stepfather's." I sat my phone on the coffee table between us and pressed the record icon.

"Hold up." He leaned over and turned it off. "Your stepfather died?"

"Yes." I pulled out the notebook I'd used on the plane, found a pen in my purse and scribbled on the back of one of the notebook pages to make sure it worked. I was in full biographer mode now.

"Why?"

"Why what? Why was it in Ohio? Or why did I go?"

"Why'd you go?"

"Because he was a good man, and I loved him." I said simply.

"Lucky you." He said, softly. "My stepfather was not a good man. Far from it."

"I'm sorry E.C."

"Yeah, well." He cleared his throat and shrugged like it didn't matter. "It is what it is. Let's talk about something else."

I started to record our conversation again, but E.C. grabbed my wrist and stared at the bandage I'd applied.

"What happened to your hand, girl?"

"Long story," I said. "Now, let's talk about how you..."

"You tell me your story, and I'll tell you mine," E.C. said. "What happened to your hand?"

"I had a run-in with an irate rooster." It came out more frustrated than I intended. I wanted to get on with the interview.

"A rooster?" E.C. let go of my wrist and leaned back. "I gotta hear this! I been to a lot of funerals, but none of them involved roosters."

Interviewing a new client is sometimes like being at a junior high dance. There's plenty of sweaty awkwardness at first, while avoiding as much eye contact as possible.

The episode with Rick's chickens might just be what I needed to put E.C. at ease. I laid my pen and notebook down.

"The rooster's name is Zedekiah..." I began. "And he was not happy when I visited his chicken kingdom without his permission."

The story of me being chased by Zedekiah, did the trick. E.C. was laughing out loud by the time I finished telling him about my attempt to gather a couple of eggs earlier that day. I pushed the record icon again, and this time he did not stop me.

I began with memories that I hoped would be happy ones. I had decided I would save the rough stuff I knew he'd been through for later.

"You play several instruments, Ezekiel. Which one was your first, and how did you get started on it?"

"Oh, wow. That takes me way back!" E.C. clasped his hand over his forehead and stared at the ceiling, remembering. "I think I was about four years old. Mama was pregnant with my little brother. Our dad had already split. Mama had gotten a job working at this small, local grocery store. It was on 8-Mile Road and close enough to walk. There was no one to watch me except this neighbor lady who lived next to us in the building. Mrs. Eddy was half-blind and hard of hearing. She should never have been put in charge of a small child, but Mama was desperate.

"I didn't have hardly any toys." He leaned forward. "But Mrs. Eddy had an old upright piano in her apartment. Someone who lived there before she moved in had left it behind, probably because it was too heavy to drag back down the four flights of steps we had to climb. That piano was out-of-tune, and a couple of the keys were stuck, but when I was four, it felt like Christmas and Disneyland all rolled up into one to me. I plunked around on that thing until most babysitters would have lost their minds, but Mrs. Eddy just smiled and thanked me for making such beautiful music for her. Sometimes I'd stand on a table and sing hymns from church, and she'd clap, and I'd be all big about myself. That's probably how I got to be the way I am. Performing all the time. You can blame Mrs. Eddy, if you want to."

I couldn't resist making a small joke. "You said she was hard of hearing?"

He laughed. "Yes, but that lady was the sweetest thing. I was lucky to have her."

I jotted a note to find out more about Mrs. Eddy.

"So, I'm curious. Did your mother pay her, or did Mrs. Eddy take care of you just out of the goodness of her heart?"

"Both. The man who owned the grocery store where Mama worked let her take home whatever overripe fruit and wilted vegetables he couldn't sell each day, in addition to her paycheck. Sometimes he'd give her a ham or beef bone with some meat still on it. Whatever he'd be throwing out. Mama wasted nothing. She'd turn all that into things like soup or pies each night when she got home, or she'd mash up the too-ripe bananas and make banana bread and she'd share it with Mrs. Eddy. We ate good!"

"What about the guitar? I've read you're practically a virtuoso on it."

"That started when I was twelve. Found it in the trash. Broken. The janitor at our building helped me repair it."

"Who taught you to play it?"

"Jackson did."

"Jackson?" I asked, my pen poised in the air.

"He was a homeless man who hung out nearby and did odd jobs when he could get them. Had a drinking problem. He only knew three chords, but he taught them to me."

"Do you still have that guitar?"

Ezekiel pointed to a case leaning against the wall. "Wouldn't go anywhere without it. Turned out it was an old Martin. Beautiful sound once I could afford to have an expert repair it."

"The flute?"

"High school band. The director gave me a loaner."

"What about the poetry? Was that from listening to other rappers?"

"Not in the beginning. I found a paperback copy of Maya Angelou's *And Still I Rise* poetry laying on the city bus and it was like a light switch went on in my head. I started trying to write my own poetry. I was a sophomore in high school and wrote a whole notebook full of bad angst-ridden nonsense. Didn't show it to no one, but it was good practice."

He seemed suddenly lost in thought, a sad, faraway look in his eyes.

"Do you still have it?"

"No. My stepfather found it."

I heard the strain in his voice. There was a story there. I'd probe it more fully later. "How did he react?"

"My stepfather was not a fan." E.C. huffed out a laugh. "Not of me. Not of my little brother. Much of the time, not even of my mother, and definitely not of my attempts at teenage poetry. I was embarrassed and made the mistake of trying to take it away from him. Ended up with a broken arm over that one."

We sat in silence. Him remembering and me digesting what he'd told me. This was heavy stuff.

"I think we're done," E.C. said, standing up abruptly.

We still had an hour left scheduled for this interview. But, if he didn't want to continue, there wasn't much I could do about it. I turned off the recording. Closed my notebook. Sometimes these interviews brought up memories that were hard to deal with. It was part of the process. It was also what I got paid to do.

"Same time tomorrow?" I asked.

E.C. sighed and nodded. "Sure."

CHAPTER 16

It took every bit of discipline I had to settle down and transcribe my notes that night after my first real interview with E.C. That wasn't like me at all! I'd always been studious to a fault. Give me a research paper to write, a test to study for, or history dates to memorize, and I was your girl. It was the only thing I was good at.

Instead of thinking about the autobiography I needed to write, though, I kept finding myself remembering my new home in Ohio and a certain Amish farmer who had promised to wait there for me to return. Lucas was taking up way too much room in my mind, and there seemed nothing I could do about it.

"You're being ridiculous!" I told my mirror as I yanked a brush through my straight brown hair before I went to bed that night. "You barely know him," I muttered, as I put lotion on my face.

Over the next few weeks, E.C. and I worked hard. We listened to most of his tracks together while he talked about the background of the music. I didn't fall in love with his music, but I respected the skill of it. There was a rawness to the images he created, accentuated by punches of unexpected rhymes and rhythms. Yet, no matter how heartbreaking the song, hope somehow always broke through at the end. That was part of E.C.'s genius.

There were almost no photos of him as a child. When I asked, he handed me the one he carried in his wallet.

"Me and my brother," he said. "Just two skinny little black kids trying to take care of each other."

Ezekiel was about twelve in the picture. He held his arm around his little brother, Michael, who was eight. They were standing in front of a brick church dressed in jeans, white dress shirts and black ties. There was nothing remarkable in the photo except for the fear in the eyes of the younger brother, and a ferocious protectiveness in Ezekiel's.

"What was going on in this picture?" I asked.

"It was the day our mother married my stepfather," E.C. said. "She couldn't see what he was, but we did. He was a different person when he was alone with us."

I handed the photo back. "You built a remarkable life despite him."

"By the sheer grace of God, yes," he said. "But I'd trade every award I've ever won, and every dime I've ever made—to have my baby brother back again."

I nodded in sympathy. The tragic loss of his brother's life in a crossfire shootout between rival gangs had been the catalyst and fuel behind E.C.'s entire career.

He cleared his throat. "Are we done here?"

"For now." I flipped my notebook close. "Any ideas for a title?"

"You'd think words would come easy for me, but I got nothing," he admitted. "So, what happens now?"

"Now, I go interview a few more people who knew you, and then I'll go write like a crazy woman until I finish this book. My deadline is December 15. Better be prepared for me to bother you with lots of fact-checking phone calls and texts."

"Call and text as much as you need."

I walked back to my apartment feeling a little less anxious about the project. I still had to write the thing, of course, but after the conversation we'd had today, I thought the book might turn out well. Maybe even really well. All I had to do was finish writing it in about half the time I needed.

And yet, when I got back to my apartment, I didn't quite know what to do with myself. I wasn't ready to write yet. I needed to let all the interviews, all the stories, simmer in my mind before I could start putting them down on paper.

I paced the floor, too wired to sit still, itching to do something besides staring out the window of my tiny apartment. That's when it hit me—now that the interviews were finished, there was nothing keeping me from driving to Rick's place. I'd have all the room I could ever want to spread out my books and notes.

I glanced at my watch. Ten o'clock, and I was wide awake. It was a seven-hour drive to Sugarcreek. If I left now and drove through the night, I'd be there before sunup—even before Zedekiah started crowing. The thought of not dealing with the hassle of LaGuardia Airport sounded appealing right now. I could make some audio notes while I drove while they were fresh in my mind.

Tomorrow I'd start typing. I'd set up in Rick's comfortable office on the main floor. Thanks to him, I now had my very own writing retreat.

Impatient to get there, I packed a suitcase and headed to my apartment's parking garage to get my six-year-old silver Camry that I seldom used. It was unusual for me to make a long trip by car, but I suddenly felt a sort of urgency. I wanted to get back there as soon as I could, just to make certain it really existed and that I hadn't made it up.

CHAPTER 17

It was unseasonably cold this morning. Lucas stood by the horse's trough, breaking up the thin skim of ice that had formed overnight. His breath fogged the chilly air.

April was usually a lovely month, but Sugarcreek had experienced an unexpected overnight cold snap. Yesterday's temperature had been in the sixties and the sun-drenched farm had been alive with honeybees busy pollinating the fruit trees and songbirds building their nests. Now, even they were hunkering down until things warmed up again. He was wondering if the tender blossoms on the peach trees had been permanently affected when he noticed headlights slowly creeping down the long driveway.

That was odd. No one from the *Englisch* world usually showed up this early, and certainly not unannounced. His muscles tensed as he watched the vehicle approach, a silver car he didn't recognize. Concern flickered in the back of his mind—who could this be? But as the car pulled closer, and the headlights swept across the driveway, he saw a tall brunette step out of the driver's seat.

It was Amy. She'd finally come back.

His heart leapt with a gladness that surprised him, though he quickly shoved it down. Feeling pleasure at the sight of an attractive *Englisch* woman was not acceptable behavior. Still, he couldn't help the slight smile that tugged at his mouth as he walked over to greet her, trying to maintain his usual solemn demeanor.

"Hi, Lucas!" Amy said as soon as she saw him, her voice forcibly bright despite the early hour. "You're up early."

"So are you," he replied, noting the tiredness in her eyes.

"I drove through the night," she said with a yawn, stretching her arms above her head. "Seemed like a good idea at the time. Halfway here, not so much."

"I am glad you made it here safely," Lucas said, the stiffness in his tone betraying the effort it took him to keep things formal.

Amy smiled. She pressed a button on her key fob, and the car trunk popped open. She struggled to pull out a suitcase that looked nearly as big as she was. Lucas stepped forward and took it from her, lifting it effortlessly.

"Thank you." Amy sounded genuinely grateful. "You make that look like it weighs nothing. I could barely wrestle it into the car."

Lucas hefted the suitcase, noting its substantial weight. "You are staying long?"

"Maybe," she said with a noncommittal shrug. She walked to the back door and stepped inside, flipping on the light as Lucas followed her in. The warm glow of Tiffany-style lamps filled the room.

"Rick's house felt like a hug the first time I walked through that door," she said, pausing in the entryway as if soaking it all in. "It still does."

"He would be pleased," Lucas choked up slightly. Rick's absence here was a void they both felt, but it was good to know his presence still lingered.

Amy shrugged off her jacket, draping it over the back of a chair. "Do you have a minute?" She pulled out a kitchen chair and sat down at the table. "I've been doing some thinking, and I want to take care of something before I start working today."

"I have some time," Lucas said, pulling out a chair and sitting across from her, his curiosity piqued.

"Do you mind explaining the details of your and Rick's business arrangement?" she asked.

"It is simple," Lucas began. "In return for living in the *Daadi Haus* and the use of the land, I pay a percentage of whatever profit I make from the farm."

Amy nodded, considering his words. "Does the farm generate enough income to offset the expenses of the place?"

"Most years, yes," Lucas said firmly. "More than enough."

"Is this farm your only income?" she asked, her tone probing.

"I do some carpentry jobs on the side," Lucas replied, tilting his head curiously. "Why do you ask?"

Amy took a deep breath. "This past week in New York, I've decided I don't want to sell. Not to anyone—even if it's not something as awful as a landfill. If nothing else, I'll use it as a writer's retreat, maybe even invite some writer friends to come to keep me company from time to time. What I'm saying is, if you wish, we can simply continue the arrangement you had with Rick. It sounds like it's worked pretty well so far."

Lucas felt like the weight of the world had been lifted from his shoulders. He'd gotten the fields ready for planting, but he'd been unsure if it was wise to spend money for seed without something more definite from Amy. The tension he hadn't even realized he was carrying dissolved. "I would like that very much,"

"Good," Amy said, as she extended her hand across the table. Lucas took it in a firm shake, the deal sealed with a simplicity that felt right.

Lucas had always believed in keeping his word. If he said he was going to do something, he did it. It was a philosophy shared by most of the local people he worked with. Honesty and reliability were the bedrock of their community. He knew he was taking a gamble trusting Amy, but somehow it seemed right.

CHAPTER 18

I'd barely gotten unpacked, when Stan paid another visit. I wondered how he even knew so quickly that I'd arrived, but I assumed realtors had their ways if the stakes were high enough. Apparently, whoever he represented wanted the land badly. He'd tried to call me several times while I was in New York, but after the first call, I didn't answer any more.

This time, he made a solid offer. I refused it and asked him to leave. He didn't. Instead, he tried to argue with me. That was a mistake. There was something about the man that grated on me. By the time he left, there wasn't a number he could have named that would have been high enough.

I stood on the porch, still fuming, as I watched Stan's black SUV disappear down the graveled driveway for the second time. Lucas stood quietly beside me. He'd heard the whole thing.

A landfill! Imagine!

"One and a half million dollars is a lot," Lucas stated quietly. "Do writers get paid so much that you can afford to pass on that offer?"

I hoped it was respect I heard in his voice—respect for the city girl who had stood her ground against those evil-doers with ugly designs on the beautiful acreage that Rick and Lucas had nurtured.

"No." I didn't hesitate. "Most of us barely make a living, if that."

"Then why do you write?"

I gave it some thought. "Because I love what I do."

Which was true.

"And I'm good at it." Which also was true.

"And because I don't have any other marketable skills," I admitted.

That was regrettably true as well.

"There will be other offers from other people." Lucas said. "There might even come a day when you feel you've received too good of an offer to refuse."

"I don't see that ever happening."

I rubbed my eyes. My overnight drive had seemed like a good idea at the time, but about two o'clock in the morning I had fallen asleep for a nanosecond and nearly ran off the road. Things had been iffy for the next few miles, with me slapping myself in the face, and singing nonsense songs to the top of my lungs to stay awake—until I saw a 24-hour Walmart sign glowing up ahead right off the interstate, like an oasis. I had pulled into the parking lot, let my seat all the way back, and slept for an hour before driving the rest of the way.

I doubted I'd ever try to do a long drive in the middle of the night again, no matter how excited I felt about a writing project. I had a suspicion that the audio notes about the book I'd been making before almost running off the road made little sense.

Climbing out of my car at Rick's in the early morning light, I'd heard Zedekiah crowing up the sun, and I felt that tug again—that indescribable sense that I was coming home. That it was a home Rick had created and saved for me made the homecoming especially sweet.

Then Stan had arrived and ruined everything. Seriously. Why couldn't he take no for an answer?

"I'm glad to hear you say that," Lucas said. "Because this land can feed many families good, healthy food. It will sustain life if treated well. People can't eat dollar bills. Someone must still till the soil and nurture the plants. Without the land, money becomes worthless."

I couldn't disagree.

"Would you like for me to show you the store now?" Lucas asked.

"Store?" I blinked in surprise. "What store?"

"Rick's store. It's in town."

"The attorney didn't mention a store," I said, my mind racing. "She just said I was to inherit this place and Rick's business—whatever that was. There's a store?"

"A very large, old store," Lucas explained, his tone matter of fact. "Filled with antiques and other nice things Rick believed to be valuable."

I took a moment to process this. "Rick would certainly know if something was valuable. He was working as an appraiser for Sotheby when my mother married him."

"Rick did not tell me that," Lucas said.

I yawned. "No one wants to turn it into a landfill, do they?"

Lucas hesitated, then asked, "Was that a joke?"

"It was, indeed, a joke." I put my hands in the air as far as I could and stretched, trying to decide what I needed most. Breakfast or a nap.

"It is good to joke together." Relief spread across his face, and I could see the tension of the morning's visit from Stan finally easing. "Would you like me to take you there?"

"Very much," I said. "But only after a couple hours' sleep, a long shower, and some breakfast."

"Then I should go about my chores until then?"

"Might as well." I headed toward the front door.

"What time do you want me to be ready to take you?" Lucas asked.

"Noon?" I suggested.

"Noon is good."

I put my hand on the doorknob.

"Before or after our noon meal?" he called.

"Lucas." I stopped and forced myself to respond with patience. "I don't care. Whatever works for you."

"Okay. Afterward, then. I will let Erma know not to bother you while you sleep."

"Thank you."

"She usually comes about ten."

"Terrific." I stepped into the house and closed the door behind me. This time, I did not sleep on the couch. I fell face down onto the bed in the guest room and lost consciousness.

CHAPTER 19

I awoke four hours later to the roar of a vacuum outside my room and the scent of bacon. The bacon was welcome, the sound of the vacuum was not. I checked my watch. It was nearly eleven thirty. I still had a half-hour to get ready before Lucas came by to go to Rick's store, or at least I thought I had a half-hour.

The vacuum switched off, and I heard a hurried consultation going on outside my door.

"Do you think she's *ever* going to get up?" Erma asked.

"I don't know," Lucas said. "But she said she wanted to go to Rick's at noon."

"Who sleeps until noon unless they are sick?" Erma said. "Was she sick?"

"She didn't seem so."

"I'm getting worried about her. Do you think I should check on her?"

As a full-time professional writer, I seldom stopped if I were on a roll unless I absolutely had to. If that meant writing until four in the morning, that's what I did. I always knew I could catch up on sleep later, but sometimes not until the first draft was finished.

I had never had anyone voicing opinions about my sleep patterns. Except my mom the few times she'd stayed with me and my typing had annoyed her.

Grateful I'd slept in my clothes, I got out of bed and yanked open the door. "I'm *fine*. Just tired from the drive."

"Are you sure that's all it is?" Erma said, concerned. "We have an *Englisch* doctor in town you could go see." A smile lit up her face. "And he's *single* too!"

Oh dear.

How sad would it be if my Amish housekeeper started trying to set me up? I was only twenty-eight. Still young, right? Finding a man wasn't high on my to-do list. Having Erma hint at matchmaking was embarrassing—especially with Lucas standing nearby.

Besides, Desiree had already tried to help me out in that regard. There was just one problem. The men my mom selected tended to fall in love with her before I could even meet them. Yeah, she was that good.

"I'm fine." I quickly changed the subject. "Is that bacon I smell?"

"I'm sure it is cold by now," Erma said. "But I will go heat it up."

I flashed back on all the mornings I'd considered myself lucky to have even a piece of cold pizza around for breakfast after Mom divorced Rick. "I can eat it cold."

"No." Erma seemed appalled at the thought. "I'll just go heat it up!"

Erma bustled off to heat my breakfast. She was a sweetheart, but I wasn't used to people being so concerned about how long I slept or when or if I ate. Erma's concern was adorable, but I wasn't sure how to deal with it.

"Perhaps now would be a good time for that shower you said you wanted?" Lucas said.

I wasn't used to having a man suggest that I should bathe, but heading into the bathroom seemed like a great idea for now.

"I'll get a few more chores finished, and then we can go," Lucas said.

"Go where?" My brain was still muddled from my nap.

"Rick's antique store."

"Right. I own an antique store. Thank you. Can't wait."

CHAPTER 20

Forty-five minutes later, I had eaten, showered, and dressed in fresh jeans and a cream-colored pleated blouse that Desiree had bought me for my last birthday. The blouse cost more than my old monthly car payment, but I wore it because it did good things for my bustline—my lack thereof being something Desiree often lamented.

My mother meant well. I determinedly believed that she always meant well. She could even be a real sweetheart sometimes, but other times she could be incredibly thoughtless. It was hard not to come away with a few low self-esteem issues when Desiree Stanton was one's mother.

The steaming mug of coffee Erma handed me as I left was so strong it threatened to curl my eyelashes.

"I thought we were taking my car," I said, stepping out onto the porch to see a horse and buggy standing ready.

"It's only two miles," he replied. "My horse needs exercise, and your car does not." He held out his hand to me, and before I knew it, I was inside the buggy, and sitting much closer to Lucas than felt comfortable.

The buggy seemed alive, bouncing around as I wedged my coffee cup between my knees and instinctively reached for a seatbelt that wasn't there.

"Most *Englisch* people do that the first time they get in," Lucas remarked with a slow grin. Then he gently slapped the reins on the rump of his horse. "Giddy-up!"

My head flew back with the sudden start, and a couple drops of coffee spilled on my knees and onto the floorboard, but the sensation of trotting down the road was exhilarating. I'd experienced nothing quite like it.

In a few minutes, we stopped in front of an ornate three-story building on Sugarcreek's Main Street. The building had an Alpine look, like the rest of the village businesses. An ornate white and gold sign read simply, "The Attic."

The building was painted cobalt blue with gingerbread trim. A hand lettered "closed" sign hung in the window. Two tourists, wearing fanny packs, their eyes shaded with their hands, were trying to peek inside.

"How long has it been closed?" I asked.

"Not long," Lucas said. "Rick worked here until the day he died. This was where he spent most of his time."

He drove the buggy around to the back of the store, where there were hitching rails. He tied up the horse and then helped me down.

Lucas unlocked the back door, letting me inside. My first impression was one of cozy clutter—antiques and the lingering aroma of coffee and old books. Victorian couches and chairs were arranged around an ornate fireplace. Good-quality old carpets covered the wooden floors, and there were knickknacks and doilies everywhere. A glass-covered counter displayed a large and varied collection of pocketknives alongside a tangled mound of jewelry.

"People have always loved coming in here," Lucas said, with quiet nostalgia. "Tourists wander in, footsore and weary. Rick always invited them to sit down, take a break, and rest their feet. In the winter, he kept a nice blaze going in the fireplace. He never minded people sitting on the furniture. If someone wanted to come in, sit down, and read a book all day, Rick was fine with that. Funny thing is, most people who came in here ended up buying something anyway, whether or not they intended to."

"It's lovely." I turned in a slow circle to take it all in.

"You haven't seen it all yet," Lucas said. "There are two more levels, plus the basement. Come, I'll show you."

The wooden stairs creaked underfoot as we made our way to the second floor. I found old photographs, antique mirrors, ancient kitchen utensils, and clothing that belonged to another century. It was overwhelming—so many things, each with its own story. It would take me a lifetime to sort through it all.

"How did Rick find this place?" I asked, as we climbed to the third floor.

"An elderly woman, a friend of his, became ill and needed to sell. Rick came to see it and ended up staying."

"Was he happy here?" I asked as we reached the top of the stairs.

"I don't know if he was happy, but he was content," Lucas said. "And he made many friends."

We emerged onto the third floor, where a vast collection of children's antique toys and dolls was displayed. But something caught Lucas's eye—a corner of the room that had been cordoned off with blankets.

"This is odd," Lucas muttered, walking over to the makeshift partition.

Behind the quilts was a disturbingly domestic scene. An old twin bed with a wooden headboard was neatly made up, sheets tucked in at the corners, and a quilt folded at the bottom. An upturned crate served as a side table, holding a stack of books. A lamp and toaster oven sat on a small table alongside a plate, a cup, and some cutlery.

"Someone is living here," Lucas said, concerned. He laid his hand on top of the toaster oven. "It's still warm."

"I'll call the police," I said, pulling my cell phone from my pocket.

"Why?" Lucas asked, looking genuinely puzzled. "Nothing of value has been disturbed."

"But you said someone is living here!"

"And I'd like to know why that person feels the need to do this," Lucas replied calmly.

"I don't think you understand." My voice rose in frustration. "Someone is staying here without permission. In New York City, we call the cops."

"And in Sugarcreek, we're more likely to be concerned about the person who is desperate enough to live like this."

"I still think we should call the police," I insisted.

"It doesn't look like whoever is living here is hurting anything. In fact, this floor looks cleaner and more organized than the last time I was here. I think I'll turn up the heat for them."

"That's crazy." I stared at him in disbelief.

"No," Lucas said, shaking his head. "It's kind. Rick would want us to see if we can help."

"But the police…"

"Don't you have a book to write?" he said.

Lucas didn't exactly shove me out of there, but in a brief time, I sat beside him clip clopping down the road back to the house, wondering what had just happened.

"Rick sometimes allowed people to stay a night or two if they were down on their luck," Lucas explained. "Just long enough for him to get some help for them. It didn't happen often, but it happened. I've not seen anyone actually move in like this before, but I'd like to deal with whoever it is, without you here."

"Even though it could be dangerous?"

"What exactly did you see in that pitiful little setup that looked dangerous to you, Amy?"

I had to admit, that corner of the room was neater than my apartment.

"I'll go talk to the person," Lucas said. "I know most of the people in Sugarcreek and am related to many of them. Perhaps it is a cousin. Perhaps I should offer them a job, since they are living in the store, anyway. Night watchman, maybe?"

"Are you serious?" I turned my head to look at him.

"A little joke." He smiled. "It is good for people to joke together. Yes?"

I let out a sigh. I was way out of my depth here in Sugarcreek, but frankly, I wanted to stick around just to see what would happen next. Even while on tour with E.C., my life didn't feel as interesting as trotting down the streets of Sugarcreek in this Amish man's buggy.

CHAPTER 21

As soon as we arrived back from The Attic, I sat my laptop, notebooks, and pens on Rick's desk. The router sat on a nearby windowsill with the password on a card next to it. I booted up my laptop and was relieved to see that the Wi-Fi signal was strong.

Erma had already gone home, leaving behind a luscious-looking apple pie. Lucas had left to go pick up some homemade shirts from his sister, and then do whatever farm stuff he needed to accomplish for the day. I intended to try to understand all that he did, but not until this Ezekiel Cross project was finished. After my four-hour nap and the buggy ride with Lucas, I adjusted the comfortable office chair, ready to write like the wind.

But as the hours ticked by, Rick's office became decidedly chilly. The office had an impressive stone fireplace, but a fire in it didn't materialize because I didn't know how to make one. I searched the house, determined to find the thermostat to the furnace, but no matter how hard I looked, I could not find it.

By late afternoon, I was shivering. I wrapped myself in a quilt, made some hot tea, found some of Rick's wool socks and layered on two pairs, but the cold seeped into my bones, making it impossible to type. I kept glancing at the clock, hoping Lucas would return. When I finally saw him coming up the driveway, I bolted out the front door, quilt and all, waving him down.

"I can't find the thermostat!" I called out, my teeth practically chattering.

"Thermostat?" He dismounted while holding a paper-wrapped package in his hand, and tied his horse to the porch railing, giving me a look that was equal parts amusement and concern. "There isn't one."

"How can you have a furnace without a thermostat?" I asked.

"There's no furnace, Amy." he said, like it was the most obvious thing in the world. "But I'll have a fire going for you in no time if you're that cold."

"I am."

"I don't think you'd feel so cold if you would go outside and walk around the sunshine for a few minutes now and then," he said. "Sitting inside at Rick's desk all day is not healthy work."

He was probably right, but who had the time to exercise? And why had he been gone so long when I was freezing to death and didn't know how to keep the house warm?

"Did you enjoy your *long* visit with your sister?" I was annoyed, and I didn't care if he knew it.

My sarcasm was lost on him.

"I did!" he said. "Very much. She has a new *bobli*! I got to rock him to sleep while she finished sewing on the last few buttons. Daniel is only ten days old and already holding his head up! He's a strong big boy, that one!"

My annoyance melted when I saw his face was alight with joy over his new baby nephew. "I'm glad your visit went so well."

I followed him to the basement, hobbled by the quilt, still bundled up like some sort of human burrito. I hadn't been down there yet, and I was surprised to find a large metal stove lurking in one corner, looking like something out of a pioneer movie.

"Living here year round, you'll need to learn how to make a fire," Lucas said, as he secured the metal door after getting a fire blazing.

"No, what I need is a proper furnace," I said, crossing my arms. "With a thermostat."

"This isn't hard to learn how to do, and I've stacked enough firewood to last you through the winter," he replied, clearly unimpressed by my protest.

I shuffled from foot to foot, waiting for the heat to reach me. "If I'm going to live here, I'll need a real furnace."

"If?" He raised an eyebrow.

"I have an apartment in New York," I pointed out, the temptation to flee back to the familiar warmth of my city life growing stronger by the minute. "It was looking real good to me while I waited for you to get back."

"Wood stoves give off a fine heat," Lucas said after a beat.

"Assuming there's an actual fire burning inside of them," I shot back.

"There's nothing to it. Once the fire is going, you just must remember to feed it with fresh firewood, so it never goes out," he explained patiently.

"How often?"

"Depends on the wood. I always get up once on cold nights to add more." He said this as if it was the most natural thing in the world.

"I'd prefer not to set an alarm in the middle of the night to keep from freezing to death," I grumbled, feeling a mix of frustration and resignation.

"You'll get used to it." Lucas's calm demeanor was unshakable, which I found irritating. "I have found it is a good time to pray while you get back to sleep."

Pray? I glanced at his face. The man was absolutely serious.

"Could you do it? You have to get up to put wood in yours, anyway. I'll pay you," I suggested, only half-joking.

He looked at me, one eyebrow raised, a hint of a smile tugging at his lips. "You're suggesting paying me to come into your house in the middle of the night to place a few sticks of firewood in the stove?"

I wrapped the quilt around me more tightly, feeling foolish but too cold to care. "Well, the way you make it sound, I guess not."

"It's a simple task. Amish women do it all the time," he said.

"And I am not an Amish woman, in case you haven't noticed."

"I've noticed."

The tone he used caused me to become instantly defensive.

"Well, Amish women don't know how to..." I searched for something, *anything*, that would prove I wasn't completely useless. "...use a subway!"

He laughed then, a genuine one that made my stomach do a little flip. "No Amish woman I know would ever want to."

"I don't care," I said. "I'm cold!"

He cocked his head to the side. "Did you go to college?"

"Of course I did."

"Where?"

"Columbia University. I have a master's degree in English. What does that have to do with anything?"

"I think there's a slight chance that even a college graduate from Columbia University with a master's degree in English might learn to toss a log on a fire to keep from freezing to death," he said. "But I might be wrong."

"Was that a joke?" I asked, narrowing my eyes at him.

"Yes, but it's also true. It is unwise to allow oneself to be incompetent," he said, his tone serious. "You can learn to do this, Amy."

The heat from the stove began to permeate my quilt. I sidled closer, savoring the warmth. "Wood heat does feel good."

"Your quilt is on fire," he pointed out.

I looked down in horror at the smoldering edge of my quilt. Lucas yanked it off me and quickly stamped out the small flame. "Please don't do that again."

"Okay," I mumbled, feeling my cheeks flush with embarrassment, grateful that I was at least modestly dressed beneath the quilt in an old gray jogging suit—the warmest thing I'd brought.

Lucas flashed me a look that was somewhere between exasperation and amusement as he headed upstairs. I trailed after him, dragging the scorched quilt behind me.

CHAPTER 22

The day after he took Amy to The Attic, Lucas left her typing away on her computer at the big desk in Rick's office as he saddled his horse and rode to the antique store. This was not his normal routine. He had plenty of other chores to do, but he was worried.

Old buildings like Rick's store required attention—water pipes could burst without warning, roofs might leak after a hard rain, and mouse traps often needed emptying. But today, his main reason for coming was to check on their uninvited guest. He'd made a point of stopping by Esther's bakery on his way so he could pick up a bag of donuts as a sort of peace offering to whoever was living there.

As soon as he opened the door, the scent of Rick's special beeswax lemon furniture polish greeted him. The walnut dining table on the first floor gleamed under the dim light, and two oak bookcases, their books freshly aligned, sparkled with a thorough dusting and polish. Someone wasn't just living there, they were apparently trying to take care of things. There was little Lucas didn't know about Rick's business, but their vagrant was a complete mystery.

Lucas's guess was it was someone Rick knew to whom he had

given a key at one time. Sometimes Rick needed help to pick up some antique furniture that he bought, or help delivering a piece that had been purchased. There was never enough work to justify actually employing someone full time for that job, but there were several men in Sugarcreek who didn't mind lending a hand for a few hours for a little extra cash. Perhaps one of them had fallen on hard times and was staying here until they could figure out what to do.

Lucas mounted the steps to the third floor, each creak of the old wooden stairs echoing in the silent building. He found the small makeshift room exactly as it had been the day before, although now there was a faint smell of food lingering in the air.

"Hello?" he called, breaking the stillness.

He waited, listening for any sign of movement. But there was nothing—no rustle, no footsteps, just the small sounds of an old building settling in on itself. His eyes were drawn to a recent addition to the little home behind the hanging blankets—a comfortable-looking overstuffed chair and footstool that hadn't been there before. Lucas remembered seeing the chair on the second floor. The little space was transforming into a home, bit by bit. It was good information to know that whoever was living here had the strength to wrestle the chair up the stairs. It validated what he had already been thinking.

"Thank you for the work you're doing," Lucas said aloud, hoping the unseen guest might be hiding and hearing him. He set the white bakery bag on the bedside table, its fresh sugary contents an offering of goodwill. "I brought some donuts from Esther's bakery if you're hungry."

Nothing stirred, although it felt as though there was life hiding behind the silence. It felt like the store was holding its breath as it watched and waited.

As he left the third floor and made his way back down to the first, Lucas's mind churned with questions. How was this person getting in and out of the building? He checked the locks again, both front and back. They were secure, no signs of tampering or forced entry. It had to be someone with a key.

One thing was certain: with the store closed, it was an excellent place to hide if someone was desperate. The thought of evicting this person, whoever they were, didn't sit well. There was something about the humble, pegged-together little space that tugged at his heart. This was someone's refuge, possibly their last grasp at having a roof over their head and some semblance of security.

He hoped Amy wouldn't force him to turn the person out, at least not yet. Not until he'd figured out who they were and what had driven them to this point. The pitiful humanness of that small, makeshift room lingered in his mind as he stepped back out into the bright afternoon light, locking the door behind him.

When he got back home, he was surprised to see Amy strolling up the driveway. She was wearing jeans and a purple t-shirt with a gray cardigan sweater tied around her waist. He dismounted when he got near her.

"Everything okay?" He took the reins in his hand and led his horse behind them.

"I took your advice," she said. "I decided it would be easier to go walking to warm myself up than try to get a fire going."

"Is it working?"

"Well, I started out wearing this sweater buttoned up to my chin, and now I wish I'd left it behind, so you tell me."

"I think the cold weather is behind us," he said. "You won't have to worry about fires until fall."

"Sure."

He could tell there was something wrong and stole a glance at her face. Her eyes were rimmed with red and her cheeks were wet. She'd been crying.

"Can you tell me what's wrong?" he asked. "Maybe I can help."

"You can't help. I'm just wishing I could go back in time and rescue Ezekiel Cross."

"Ezekiel is the person you are writing about? He needed rescuing?" His horse decided it needed to eat a luscious-looking clump of grass beside the fence. Lucas stopped to let it, and Amy paused her walk as well.

"When he was a child, yes," Amy said. "And his little brother as well."

"So, this writing about his life is hard on you?"

"It has to be," Amy said. "I must feel what he felt as much as possible so I can write it accurately. Otherwise, the writing won't do justice to what he went through. Readers won't understand."

He looked at her tear-stained face, and for the first time, he saw her through fresh eyes. She was more than just some *Englisch* woman who sat around all day typing on a computer for a living. What she did was hard, and it took an emotional toll on her.

"I hate feeling sad. Especially about things I can't fix." She scrubbed her face with both hands and then smiled at him. "Let's change the subject. Catch me up. Is there still a vagrant living in Rick's antique store?"

"Yes."

"And you still don't feel it necessary to let the police know what's going on?"

"They aren't hurting anything," Lucas explained. "In fact, I think they're trying to pay you back."

Amy tilted her head, intrigued. "How?"

"Some of the furniture has been dusted and polished. The merchandise is more organized. If you leave this visitor alone, I think you're going to have a much neater store from them staying there."

"Interesting. I'll trust your decision on this for now," Amy said. "It's going to take everything I can do to finish the book on time. I don't think I can deal with anything else."

"When do you think you'll reopen the store? Or do you plan to?"

Amy sighed. "Lucas, I don't know the first thing about running a store, but I also know I don't want to sell it. At least not yet. Can we just not do anything with it until I finish the book?"

"Amy, it's your store, not mine. You can do anything you want with it. But it appears that you have some sort of caretaker staying there, whether or not you want them. Do you mind if I leave them alone for now?"

"Do what you think best, Lucas," she said. "I really have to get back to work now. I'm sorry."

"Not a problem." He watched her go back inside, then a few moments later, when he passed the house, he saw her in the window of Rick's office typing on her computer again. He wondered how she stood it, this job of hers.

If he had to stay inside all day, week after week, in front of a computer, it would just about kill him. He loved working outdoors, especially on a day like today! The cold snap had lasted less than twenty-four hours. Today the temperature felt downright balmy—at least it did to him. The fruit trees had recovered, and the bees were magically turning nectar into honey; the birds were filling their nests with their perfect little eggs, all while the earth practically shouted glory to God!

He was humbled and grateful to get to be part of the celebration of living things as he walked toward the fields, making plans about what to plant next in the rich soil.

CHAPTER 23

The days blurred together as I fought my way toward the deadline. Every morning, I sat up my laptop, notebooks, and favorite pens on Rick's oversized mahogany desk. It sat right beneath the window that looked out over the driveway. I couldn't have asked for a better office.

The room was everything I'd ever dreamed of. Floor-to-ceiling bookcases packed with an eclectic mix of books lined one entire wall, and two comfy chairs flanked a stone fireplace that promised warmth and comfort come fall, if I could talk Lucas into teaching me how to build a fire in it.

As spring turned into summer, I learned that not only did Rick's house lack a furnace, it also did not have air conditioning. This was a shock to me. I had never lived without air conditioning, even in the poorest places Mom and I had stayed.

Erma suggested I try opening the windows and letting my body adjust naturally to the outdoor temperature. She pointed out that all the large trees kept the house well shaded. I disliked the idea, but I disliked trying to find someone to install air conditioning even more.

It would create a major disruption in the house and be a major distraction.

I told Erma I would try it her way. She smiled and kept me well-supplied with iced tea.

Each day, no matter how late I stayed up writing, I couldn't wait to dive back into my work in the morning, to lose myself in the words and stories that needed to be written.

But this morning, as soon as I settled into my chair, I caught sight of Lucas out the window. He was leaving on horseback again, and for a moment, I lost my train of thought, mesmerized by the way he handled the horse with such effortless skill.

I mentally slapped myself—there was no time for distractions. There was no room in my deadline for admiring attractive farmhands or marveling at the way a true horseman rode his horse.

I went into the kitchen, poured myself another glass of iced tea, brought it back to my desk, and focused on my computer. There was a story to be told, and I thought it could be an important one. There wasn't much chance that kids growing up in situations like Ezekiel and his brother would read the book, but Hollywood was already showing interest, and street kids did watch movies.

Done well, this book about Ezekiel's life might make a small difference to someone. Those were the thoughts that drove me as I chose the words that would tell the Cross brothers' story.

CHAPTER 24

M y agent called the first of July to tell me that E.C.'s new album was coming together faster than expected. Because of this, they were rushing to put together another tour for him. Of course, they needed his autobiography to come out in time for the tour. They wanted to know if I could complete the manuscript by December 15. I told my agent no. There was no way. My agent told me I really needed to say yes career-wise. She had never steered me wrong, so feeling sick at heart, I said yes.

I now had only six months left to finish the book. This was crazy. It wasn't enough time.

I could legally hold them to the original contract, but I had money issues to consider. I'd gotten a third of my advance when I first signed the contract and wouldn't get the second third until I handed in the completed manuscript. The final third would be paid when the book was actually published.

This would not have been a problem except that although Rick had left me a couple million dollars' worth of property, he had left little in the way of money in the bank. As Erma pointed out, like many of the Amish in the area, I was "land rich and cash poor." The faster I got a finished manuscript into the publisher's hands, the better for everyone.

I had already sublet my apartment to a friend. She was happy to live in a prime location, and I was happy I didn't have to pay rent, but I still needed money to live on. The way I saw it, I had four options. Ask my mother for a loan (I wasn't sure she'd give me one), put the farm or antique store up for sale (which would break my heart) or I could write like my hair was on fire. I chose to write like my hair was on fire.

Weeks passed in a blur of words. Besides a few fitful hours of sleep each night, the only relief I allowed myself was each day when Lucas insisted I leave my desk and take a twenty-minute walk.

Reluctantly, I agreed, mainly because I'd heard the horror stories of other writers who had developed major health problems because of a writing schedule like the one I was keeping. I walked with him, but I set a timer on my phone. I went back to work as soon as my twenty minutes were up.

Lucas sometimes had outdoor things to show me, like the tender new shoots in the vegetable garden, or a newborn calf, or a nest of baby birds begging for food. Sometimes we talked about the story I was writing. He often surprised me with his insight. That's how I discovered, like Ezekiel, he also had lost a younger brother—to a farming accident.

Summer passed too quickly, and fall came rushing at me like an out-of-control freight train. In September, three Amish children began taking a shortcut through our farm to their one-room schoolhouse down the road.

The littlest girl had trouble keeping up. The others did not go off and leave her alone. Even with children, that was not the Amish way. But Lucas always seemed to be watching when they came. He would sweep her up into his arms and carry her the rest of the way, chatting with the other children as they walked.

In my world, non-related men did not pick up little girls without getting into serious legal trouble. Concerned, I questioned him about the wisdom of it. He looked at me like I was speaking a foreign language.

"Little Sarah was born prematurely, and her growth has not yet caught up. It is difficult for her to walk so far. Her mother is heavily pregnant and needs to stay close to home. Why would my sister object to me walking her *kinder* to school?"

Oh.

I had only one relative that I knew of—my mother. It was hard to wrap my mind around the life of a man with five sisters, twenty-seven nephews and nieces, and an incomprehensible number of cousins. The invisible web of relationships in Amish country was a wonder and a mystery to an outsider like me, but I was beginning to understand enough to be a little envious.

Fall melted into winter as I pushed into self-edits. Every time I thought about the deadline, my chest tightened with panic.

The beauty directly outside my window helped calm me down. Lucas had installed a bird feeder, and he kept it well-stocked. Cardinals and bluejays and many others became my companions, fluttering and chirping, their bright colors a stark contrast to the bare branches and the early dustings of snow.

I'd pause from time to time, watching them dart back and forth. They were like tiny bursts of joy, reminding me that there was still a world out there beyond the pages over which I was obsessing.

But as the deadline loomed closer, the pressure mounted even more, turning my days into a desperate battle against the clock. I stopped going on the walks with Lucas because it took too long to suit up against the cold. My only form of exercise devolved into trips to the bathroom. I'm not sure who kept the fire going. Erma and Lucas, I suppose. All I know is that it wasn't me.

I knew vaguely that Erma came and went, often bringing a grand-baby or one of her grown daughters along. It seemed important to her that every member of her family meet Rick's "daughter," the writer. No one bothered with the "step" before "daughter" anymore and honestly, I was fine with that.

I greeted them in a kind of apologetic fog, my mind half in the room with them and half in the world I was creating. They seemed to understand the pressure of a work deadline, even if they didn't fully grasp the specifics of writing one's soul into a manuscript.

Other neighbors stopped by as well, popping in to say hello and to welcome me to Sugarcreek. Erma had warned them that I was in the middle of a major writing project, so they didn't stay long. I appreciated the gesture. There was something comforting about neighbors who cared enough to check on me. Lucas—God bless him—whenever he was around, he'd smoothly take over the conversation after a few minutes, giving me a chance to retreat into my work.

Those brief interactions were not an annoyance, they were a lifeline, pulling me back from the brink of the terrible loneliness that always seemed to accompany the final stages of a major writing project. Usually, I'd shut myself up in my apartment, avoiding all human contact for fear of losing my momentum. But here, in Rick's house, there was life all around me, a community going about their work while quietly cheering me on.

Lucas checked on me often throughout the day, bringing with him the crisp scent of winter air and the earthy smells of farm work. Every time he entered the house, it was literally a breath of fresh air, grounding me when the words on the screen blurred. His presence was like the steady rhythm of a strong heartbeat that contrasted with the frantic pace of my writing.

CHAPTER 25

L ucas had known plenty of hard-working women in his life. His mother, his sisters, his late wife—they all knew how to work, but they also knew when to stop, when to take a breath and enjoy the small pleasures of life. They balanced work with moments of rest, laughter, and play. But Amy was different. She took work to a level that bordered on fanaticism. From what he could tell, she barely slept and ate only as an afterthought.

At first, he tried not to interfere. It wasn't his place to tell a grown woman how to live her life. But as the days passed, his concern grew. He'd catch glimpses of her through the window of Rick's office— sometimes wearing a coat as she sat hunched over her computer, fingers flying across the keyboard. That coat meant she'd let the fire go out. Again. Honestly, the woman needed a keeper.

It wasn't long before Lucas took matters into his own hands. He started letting himself into the house several times a day, quietly stoking the fire and making sure she had food and drink at her elbow. She was too immersed in her work to notice much, and if she did, she said nothing. Her mind was clearly locked in some creative struggle that drove her to push herself beyond what he thought was healthy.

Winter always lightened his workload, and Lucas found himself with some free time. Aside from feeding the livestock and taking on a few local carpentry jobs, he had hours to fill, and increasingly, he spent them inside Rick's house. It started to feel natural to sit in the office, borrowing a book from Rick's well-stocked shelves while he monitored the fire and Amy. She barely acknowledged him. Typing furiously one moment, pacing the room, muttering to herself, the next.

He knew Rick would have wanted someone to watch over her, to make sure she didn't burn herself up or fall ill from sheer exhaustion. So, he took on the role of silent guardian, making sure she stayed warm and fed, occasionally enlisting the help of neighbors who had become just as fascinated with Rick's daughter's writing process as he had.

Amy seemed uninterested in finding out any more about the trespasser living in the antique store. Nor was she interested in having any sort of discussion about opening it up for business and hiring someone to run it.

"Later," she said the one time he'd brought it up. "After the book is finished. We can talk about it then. I can't think about any of that now."

Lucas went to The Attic once a week, but whoever was living there was always gone, or more likely, hiding. He'd leave some food for them, thank them for cleaning the place up in case they were in earshot, and then he'd leave. He also kept the heat turned up. When he'd come back, the food would be gone, and another corner of the store would be tidied. Sometimes some small domestic comfort would have been added to the shabby world that had been created behind the soft walls created by hanging up blankets.

At one point, the person had apparently unearthed some old oil paints and brushes. With no real canvases to use, they'd painted pictures directly onto the bare wall, and then cleverly hung empty discarded frames on top of them to look as though they were framed works of art.

Although Lucas was no artist, the paintings seemed well done to him. All were of scenes from directly outside the windows of the antique store. There were no clues about the artist—nothing personal that might give a clue who they were or where they were from.

As the days passed, Lucas dipped into Rick's library more often. He'd never been much of a reader, but with his self-appointed duty to keep Amy from freezing or starving, he had plenty of time to explore the books that lined the walls. Rick, who had become a member of a Mennonite church later in life, had a collection that included modern translations of the Bible, along with a few commentaries. Lucas found himself drawn to these.

But this newfound interest led him to make a colossal error in judgment. Fascinated by what he was learning, Lucas decided to talk to his bishop, Elmer Yoder, about the passages he'd found so interesting. He and Elmer had always gotten along. It seemed like a harmless idea, sharing spiritual insights with Elmer that had struck him so deeply.

The conversation did not go as planned. Elmer's reaction wasn't just dismissive; it was fearful. When Lucas tried to show him the passages, Elmer recoiled, as though the book itself might bite. "Nein," the bishop said, firmly. "You must read only from our German Bible."

Lucas frowned. "The language the German Bible uses is over five hundred years old. The language is so archaic I can barely understand it. Can you?"

Elmer's expression shifted to one of shock, and he took a step back, as if Lucas had uttered something blasphemous. In the silence that followed, Lucas realized he had crossed a line. Challenging the bishop's defense of the use of Martin Luther's Bible wasn't just unwise. It was dangerous, and he wasn't certain what the fallout might be.

CHAPTER 26

A foot of snow was predicted overnight, a sure sign that winter had fully settled into Sugarcreek. As Lucas stood in the barn's doorway, listening to the quiet, snow-muffled world outside, it occurred to him that if Amy parked her car in the barn alongside his buggy, he wouldn't have to clean it off later if she needed to go somewhere. The barn was warm and dry—just the place to keep her vehicle safe from the elements.

He decided to go inside and suggest it to her, but when he entered the house, he found her asleep on the couch. She was curled up beneath a thick quilt, her breathing soft and steady.

Her car keys dangled from a hook by the door, and Lucas hesitated. He knew how to drive; he still had a driver's license from his *Rumspringa* days, a relic of a time when he'd been allowed to test certain boundaries within his faith. Like many other Amish men and women, he kept his license up to date, not because he intended to use it, but because it was handy as an ID. He knew the practical side of him would regret not putting the car away when the snow piled up. And besides, it was a simple act of kindness, one he was sure Rick would have appreciated.

Unwilling to wake her, Lucas decided to park the car in the barn himself. He slipped the keys off the hook, careful not to make a sound, and stepped outside into the frosty night. Snowflakes were already beginning to fall, thick and fast, as he slid into the driver's seat of Amy's car. The interior was chilly, but the engine roared to life with a turn of the key. He took a moment to adjust to the feel of the vehicle— it had been a long time since he'd driven, but the motions came back to him easily.

Just as he was about to back out of the driveway, the headlight of an approaching buggy caught his eye. His heart sank as he recognized the figure in the driver's seat—Bishop Elmer Yoder. Of all the times for the bishop to drop by, this had to be the worst. Being caught by the bishop while sitting behind the steering wheel of a running car was the kind of scenario that could cause all sorts of trouble. In his Amish community, driving a car was nearly as looked down on as having electricity. If anything could raise suspicion, this was it.

Lucas watched as the bishop's expression shifted from surprise to stern disapproval. The look on Elmer's face was enough to tell Lucas that this would not be an easy conversation. Sighing, he turned off the car, stepped out, and walked over to the bishop's buggy, the snow crunching under his boots.

"Can I help you, Elmer?" Lucas asked, trying to keep his tone neutral.

"Yes," the bishop said, sharply. "You can explain what you are doing inside that *Englisch* woman's vehicle?"

Lucas knew he had to tread carefully. "I was just pulling it into the barn," he said calmly. "Erma mentioned this morning that we're supposed to get at least a foot of snow overnight. I didn't want it buried by morning."

"Why is she not performing this chore for herself?" the bishop asked, his tone growing more suspicious.

"She's sleeping right now," Lucas replied, keeping his voice steady. "I didn't want to wake her."

The bishop's eyebrows shot up, his expression hardening. "And how do you know this woman you are not married to is sleeping?"

Lucas cursed himself internally for his choice of words. It had been an innocent remark, but anything he said now would sound defensive. He straightened his shoulders and met the bishop's gaze head-on. "I have done no wrong, Elmer," he said firmly. "I'm just being a good neighbor and employee. That is all."

The bishop wasn't satisfied. "Being a good neighbor to this *Englisch* woman is not shunning evil. It is creating a path for it. You must be very careful, Lucas. You should find yourself a good Amish wife. Then an *Englisch* woman would not be such a temptation."

"She's not a temptation, Bishop," Lucas said, a hint of frustration creeping into the tone of his voice. "She's just someone who needs a little help."

"You are lying to yourself," Elmer replied. "And you are lying to me. I suggest you pray hard that you are not led astray."

Lucas bit back the retort that sprang to his lips, thoughts of defending Amy's character swirling in his mind. The bishop was turning Amy into something she wasn't, a figure of temptation, when she was simply a woman trying to survive. But Lucas knew better than to say these thoughts out loud.

"Here," the bishop handed him a book from Rick's library that Lucas had taken him a few days earlier, hoping to discuss it. "I do not need to read this *Englisch* foolishness."

The book was *Mere Christianity* by C.S. Lewis, and reading had felt like he'd opened a window through which fresh air had flowed into a stuffy room.

Lucas nodded stiffly and watched as Elmer turned his buggy around, the wheels cutting through the fresh layer of snow.

"Did you even try to read it?" Lucas knew he'd stepped over a line the instant the words came out of his mouth.

"Whoa!" Elmer stopped his horse and leaned out to face Lucas. "I have grown weary of your rebellious attitude! I am placing you under

Meidung for the next six months. You should spend that time in prayer and repentance instead of reading so many *Englisch* books and driving that *Englisch* woman's vehicle."

As Lucas stood there with snowflakes catching in his hair and melting on his skin, he knew that, even though he had done no wrong, Bishop Elmer Yoder would not let go of this. With a sigh, he turned back to Amy's car, easing it into the barn as he had planned.

CHAPTER 27

It was nearly three in the morning when my phone rang. Fortunately, I was awake and working. I grabbed it up off the desk, dropped it, nearly fell off the chair retrieving it, and saw that it was from Desiree.

"Hi, Mom," I said. "Where are you?"

It had been weeks since I'd heard from my mother, which wasn't unusual for us. We went for long stretches without communicating, especially when one of us was deep in a project. It also wasn't unusual when she did call for it to happen at all hours of the night. Desiree didn't bother figuring out time zones. Wherever she was at the moment seemed to be the only reality for her. She assumed other people should just deal with it.

"Vienna," her voice came through the line, as crisp as ever. "We just wrapped up filming. Where are you?"

"I'm at Rick's," I replied, my eyes scanning the last paragraph I'd written. A skipped word caught my attention, and I quickly added it, trying to stay in the flow.

"You sound distracted. What are you doing?"

"Finishing Ezekiel Cross's autobiography," I said, hoping she'd show at least a flicker of interest.

"Who?" she asked, her tone flat.

"The rapper. Ezekiel Cross," I repeated. "I told you all about it when I first got the job."

"I don't remember that. Why on earth are you writing an autobiography for a rapper?" she asked.

"The original autobiographer couldn't complete the project, and my agent got me in on it. It's kind of a big deal. He's going on tour again in March and my book…"

She cut me off. "Oh, never mind. I don't really care about that right now."

"Not a big surprise, Mom," I muttered. I leaned back in Rick's office chair, feeling that familiar wave of frustration wash over me I often felt when trying to communicate with Desiree. "But I think it's going to be one of the best books I've—"

"You aren't still considering keeping that place, are you?" she interrupted.

That old sick feeling began like it always did whenever she disapproved of one of my decisions.

"It's beautiful here, and the people are so kind—"

"It's in the middle of nowhere, darling," she cut in again.

"That's one reason I like it, Mom."

"It is not good for you to hide away," she lectured, her voice taking on that familiar tone that made me feel like a slow learner. "You know how you are. Give you a book to read or to write, and you'll never come up for air. It's things like this that are turning you into an old maid."

Seriously? Did anyone use terminology like that anymore? "I'm only twenty-eight."

"Is it that Lucas fellow?" Her eyes turned sly, as though she'd just uncovered a big secret. "He is quite attractive, but Amy, he's Amish!" she said, dropping her tone to one she used when scolding her toy poodle, "What on earth would you ever talk with him about? Pigs and horses?"

I felt a slow burn in the pit of my stomach. She had no idea who Lucas really was, how deeply he thought, how voraciously he read.

"Lucas is my friend," I said, trying to keep my words even. "And yes, he's Amish, which means he would never be interested in me. From what I understand, the Amish never marry outside their church."

"So, you *are* interested in him," she crowed, seizing on my words.

"I'm not," I insisted, though I knew it sounded like a lie even to my own ears.

"Nothing can be done until spring anyway," she said, her voice dripping with mysterious satisfaction. "So, you may as well stay at Rick's until then."

A wave of suspicion washed over me. "What does that mean?"

"Oh, I have a little something up my sleeve that will thrill you," she said, her voice brimming with self-satisfaction. "Think of it as my Christmas present to you."

"What have you done, Mother?" A sinking feeling settled in my gut.

"Nothing but good," she replied, the false innocence in her voice only making my anxiety worse. "You'll see. But I must get off the phone now."

The call ended, leaving me staring at the phone. If there was one thing I knew for sure from harsh experience—a surprise from Desiree seldom turned out well for anyone but her.

CHAPTER 28

Lucas's frustration burned hot as his horse trotted steadily home. There was simply no reasoning with Bishop Elmer Yoder, and Lucas was upset with himself for even trying. He had gone to the bishop's home hoping to get him to rescind his decision about placing him under the *Meidung*, but the discussion had spiraled.

What he had intended to be a thoughtful conversation turned into a half-hour of unproductive back-and-forth, with Bishop Yoder growing more rigid and defensive by the minute.

Bishop Yoder was a righteous and good man. Lucas knew that. But while the bishop seemed to see the Bible in stark black and white, Lucas was starting to see it in vibrant color.

There was so much hope, so much freedom and grace within its pages! But embracing new ideas wasn't a strong suit for the Amish, especially not for bishops like Elmer, who bore the weight of their settlement's souls on their shoulders and always took what they thought was the safest choice.

Still, it was humiliating to be shunned—even for just six months— when he had done nothing wrong. All he had done was study the

Bible, ask a few questions, and try to be a helpful neighbor to Rick's daughter, who was also his employer.

With a determined sigh, Lucas jammed his hat back on his head and told his horse to giddy-up. If he was going to be under a six-month ban, he'd just have to make the best of it. There was no use dwelling on it now.

On his way home from the bishop's, Lucas stopped by the antique store once again to check on their invisible visitor and make sure the heat was still on. The temperature had dropped to below zero last night, and the last thing he wanted was frozen pipes or a frozen guest.

As he let himself into the store, the first thing he noticed was that the long glass counter in the front had been polished to a sparkly shine. The large mound of tangled necklaces, earrings, and bracelets that had been there a week ago were now neatly sorted and displayed.

Whoever their visitor was, they were a hard worker, and he respected that.

Once again, Lucas mounted the creaky wooden steps to the third floor, his curiosity piqued. This time, he had brought a large slice from a lemon pound cake Erma had made for Amy.

As he reached the top of the stairs, he noticed that something else had changed. An old-fashioned plastic radio, turned low, was playing Christmas music in the corner. A raggedy-looking fake Christmas tree sat nearby, decorated with mismatched ornaments that looked like they'd been scavenged from around the building.

Then he saw him—a teenage boy, maybe seventeen or eighteen, lay curled up under a heavy blanket. He was wearing Amish clothing, his face flushed and feverish. When he looked up at Lucas, there was a desperate hope in his eyes.

"I prayed you would come," the boy said, his voice weak and strained. "I am very sick."

Lucas felt a surge of alarm as he laid the back of his hand against the boy's forehead. The heat radiating from the boy's skin was alarming. "You're burning up." Lucas tried to keep his voice calm, even as his mind raced with concern.

"Thirsty," the boy whispered, his cracked lips barely moving as he spoke. His eyes were glassy with fever.

Lucas quickly checked the pitcher on the bedside table, but it was bone dry. "I'll get you some water," he said, his voice steady, though inside, he was rattled. "Then we'll get you to a doctor."

"No!" The boy's eyes flew open with fear as he struggled to sit up, grabbing Lucas's arm with surprising strength for someone so sick. "Please, no doctor!"

"Okay." Lucas soothed him. He placed a hand on the boy's shoulder to ease him back down onto the bed. "Just rest for now. We'll talk about it later."

The boy relaxed slightly, his grip loosening as sick exhaustion took over. Lucas wasted no time; he ran downstairs, his boots thudding against the wooden steps, the empty pitcher clutched in his hand. He filled it quickly at the bathroom sink, his mind racing as he tried to figure out what to do next.

With the pitcher full, Lucas rummaged through the drawers behind the counter, searching for the bottle of Tylenol he knew Rick always kept there. He found it, then grabbed a washcloth, wetting it beneath the bathroom faucet, before racing back upstairs.

When Lucas returned, he propped the boy up gently, poured water into a glass, and held it to the boy's lips as he gulped, his body trembling with effort. Lucas then handed him the Tylenol, and the boy swallowed two capsules. After laying him back down, Lucas placed the cool washcloth on his forehead, hoping the medicine would kick in soon.

"How long have you been sick?" Lucas asked, his voice gentle as he sat beside the bed, watching the boy's labored breathing.

"Two days," the boy murmured, his eyes fluttering shut as if even speaking those two words had drained him.

"What's your name?" Lucas asked, though he wasn't sure if the boy would respond.

There was a long pause, and Lucas wondered if he had fallen asleep. But then the boy's lips moved, barely a whisper. "John Yoder."

"Where are you from, John?" Lucas asked, leaning in to catch the boy's faint voice.

Another long silence. "Pennsylvania," John finally answered. "I came looking for my cousins, but they moved. I don't know where... and I have no more money."

Lucas's heart sank. A young boy, barely more than a child, sick and alone in a strange place with no family or friends. Why hadn't he contacted a local Amish church? He should know that his people would help, whether or not they were blood kin. "Who are your cousins?"

"Henry and Sam Yoder," John said, his voice trailing off. Such common Amish names. There were probably hundreds of Henry and Sam Yoders spread across Ohio in various Amish settlements. Finding his cousins could be like finding a needle in a haystack.

"How did you get in here?" Lucas asked.

"The back door lock isn't strong," John admitted after a moment. "It takes only a little shake to make it open."

Lucas nodded, filing that information away for later. Then, he switched to Pennsylvania Deutsch, asking John about the Amish church he was part of back in Pennsylvania. John closed his eyes and didn't respond. Lucas had the feeling the boy had used up what strength he possessed answering the few questions Lucas had already asked.

Sitting there, listening to the boy's shallow breathing, Lucas felt a surge of protectiveness mixed with helplessness. He couldn't just leave the boy here, but what was he supposed to do? Taking him to a doctor was apparently out of the question, and he wasn't sure how long he could care for someone this ill without help.

CHAPTER 29

I forced myself to stop self-editing and polishing the completed manuscript. There would be more work to do once my editor scrubbed through it, but for now I had hit my deadline.

I did not know if it was any good or not. I didn't know if Ezekiel would like or hate it. All I knew was that I had done the very best I knew how, and my time was up.

My body felt like a fist that had been clenched so tightly for so long that it had forgotten how to relax. Every muscle in my back and neck burned from hunching over the computer. I knew this feeling from other writing marathons—the sense of having just emerged from a long illness, the fog that clouded my thoughts, the physical weariness.

The most significant hurdle to me was to see if E.C. liked it. That part of the ghost-writing process was always the most nerve-wracking. Writing about someone's life was a lot like painting their portrait. People wanted to look good, to see themselves reflected in a way that was both true and flattering.

I hoped that E.C. would approve of the title I'd chosen. It was based on something he'd said when he'd shown me the photo of him and his brother as children. He'd talked about how he had chosen the right rhythm for his rap. When he said he always heard the beat of his brother's heart in his head when he was rapping, I knew I had a title. *The Beat of My Brother's Heart* felt right to me. I had already suggested the cover artist use the photo E.C. had shown me, the one with fear in his little brother's eyes.

With a deep breath, I pushed "send." My email made that familiar celebratory "whooshing" sound as the tentatively titled manuscript shot off to my editor, my agent, and Ezekiel. It was out of my hands now. However, even as I tried to shift my focus, the future loomed large in my mind. What would I do if E.C. hated it?

I stood up, stretching my sore muscles, and walked over to the window. The late afternoon light cast long shadows across the snow-covered yard.

I needed to find something to occupy my mind, something to distract me from the endless possibilities of what could go wrong. Maybe I should take a walk, let the crisp winter air clear my head. Maybe I'd tackle that stack of books on Rick's bedside table that I'd been eyeing ever since I arrived. Or maybe I'd go see if Lucas was doing anything interesting. I desperately needed a distraction to help keep the doubts at bay.

CHAPTER 30

A half-hour after getting the water and Tylenol, Lucas saw John's eyelids flutter open. He placed his hand on the boy's forehead. Relief washed over him when he felt the coolness that signaled the fever had finally broken. The combination of hydration and Tylenol had worked, although he still looked pale and fragile.

"Do you need more water?" Lucas asked.

John nodded weakly. Lucas reached for the pitcher he'd filled earlier and poured a glass. As he handed it to the boy, he noticed how John's hands trembled as he took it. Thank goodness he'd chosen to stop by.

"I brought some pound cake from home," Lucas said. "We'll get you something more nutritious later, but you must be hungry. Would you like a few bites now?"

"*Danke*," John murmured, his voice hoarse but grateful. He began to eat and drink, taking small, cautious bites, as though unsure if his body could handle the food.

Lucas was interested in the way John talked. The few words of Pennsylvania Deutsch the boy sprinkled into his speech had an accent that was unfamiliar—different from the dialects spoken around

Sugarcreek. It added another layer to the mystery of this boy's background. Who was he really? Where had he come from? And what had driven him to end up alone and sick in an old, drafty antique store?

Lucas watched him closely. The boy needed more than just food and water. He needed warmth, safety, and someone to watch over him until he regained his strength. It made little sense to leave him here in the store, where the cold would continue to seep in through the cracks even with the heat cranked up. Taking him home to the *Daadi Haus*, where he could keep a closer eye on him, seemed like the best option.

"Will you call the police?" John asked suddenly, his voice small, as though he feared the answer. "I heard that woman who came the first time say that's what she wanted to do."

"No," Lucas said firmly, shaking his head. "You've done no harm here. If anything, you've left this place better than you found it. I doubt the police have ever seen someone break into a place and leave it tidier than it was before. They'd probably want to hire you."

A ghost of a smile flickered across John's face, the first sign of anything resembling hope or humor since Lucas had found him. "I'm not lazy," John said. His voice held a hint of pride.

"And that's a good thing," Lucas replied, nodding in approval. "But how did you manage to feed yourself all this time?"

"*Joe's Home Plate* down the street," John answered, his voice gaining a little more strength as he spoke. He shifted slightly, pulling himself up until his back was supported fully by the old-fashioned headboard. "I go every night after they close to see what they've thrown out. Often, it's still warm."

Lucas's heart sank at anyone having to scavenge for food in the night, digging through the trash like an animal. He knew Joe and Rachel Matthias, the couple who owned the restaurant. They were kind-hearted, generous people who would be devastated to know that a teenager had been feeding himself out of their garbage.

"I know the people who own the place. There's a sign on their door that says if you're hungry and have no money, you can still eat —no questions asked," Lucas said. "Why didn't you tell them you needed food? They would have welcomed you and given you a meal."

John looked down at his hands, his expression a mix of shame and stubbornness. "I didn't want to ask for food every day. Besides, what they throw out is better than what I've been used to eating at home."

Lucas blinked in surprise. He had never known an Amish boy to say something like that. If there was one thing Amish families took pride in, it was their ability to provide hearty, nourishing meals. That John didn't want to return home spoke volumes about the conditions he had left behind.

Lucas thought carefully before speaking again. This boy, this stranger who had appeared out of nowhere, needed more than just a warm bed and a full belly. He needed someone to show him genuine compassion.

"Where did you say you were from again?" Lucas asked, again.

"Pennsylvania."

"Where exactly in Pennsylvania?"

"Lancaster."

"Who are your people?" Lucas asked. "I have some relatives from Lancaster I go to visit sometimes. Maybe I could take you back there, since your visit with your cousins didn't turn out like you'd hoped. What's your father's name?"

There was a long hesitation while John took his time adjusting his suspenders. "Paul Yoder."

Interesting. It would be hard to come up with a more common Amish name. Lucas could name at least five Paul Yoders just among the Sugarcreek Amish.

"Would you like for me to make arrangements to help you get home?"

"I'd rather stay here for now." John spoke too quickly.

The kid might be a runaway. Sometimes there was trouble at home

141

—even in an Amish home. Amish fathers sometimes leaned too hard on teenage sons for heavy field labor.

Lucas put away further questions for now. The one thing he was certain of was the boy's need to be watched and cared for. "If you think you're strong enough to walk down the stairs," Lucas began, "I'll take you home with me. I have an extra bedroom. It'll be easier to care for you there. Would you like that?"

John looked up at Lucas, his eyes wide and vulnerable. There was a long pause before he answered, as though he was afraid to hope for such kindness. But when he finally spoke, his voice was thick with emotion. "I would like that very much."

"Then let's get you home." Lucas helped John to his feet, steadying him as he put on his hat and coat. As they made their way down the stairs, he wondered what might come next. This boy was a mystery Lucas was determined to unravel. He felt a growing sense of unease. Something was very wrong here, but first, he intended to help him get well.

CHAPTER 31

Lucas shook the snow off his boots, stomping to dislodge the last stubborn clumps, before stepping through the kitchen door. The warmth of Rick's house enveloped him like a comforting blanket. The scent of homemade cooking hung in the air, mingling with the faint aroma of wood smoke from the fire he'd stoked earlier. As he hung his coat on the peg by the door, he noticed Amy standing in front of the open refrigerator, her brow furrowed in confusion.

She stared into the fridge as if it held the secrets of the universe. Containers of lasagna, bowls of fruit salad, and a neatly sliced roast covered in plastic wrap sat on the refrigerated shelves. She blinked at the abundance of food, as though trying to piece together how it had all gotten there.

From what he had observed, her life the last few days had been a blur of editing, last-minute phone calls to Ezekiel for fact checks, fifteen-minute naps, and surviving on caffeine and the occasional snack.

"You're not at your desk," Lucas said. "Is the book finished?"

"For now." She pulled a dish of lasagna and a bowl of fruit salad out of the refrigerator. "I'm finished until I get the edits back. But where did all this food come from?"

"The lasagna is from Erma's oldest daughter, Rose." Lucas leaned against the kitchen counter. "Erma has been worried about you. She told her daughters how you were struggling to meet your deadline, and they've been bringing you food every evening."

Amy looked at him, her eyes wide with surprise. "People I barely know have been taking care of me. Why?"

"Because you were in a work crisis," Lucas explained, his tone matter of fact. "My people help one another when someone has too much to do. Since they couldn't help you write the book, they fed you."

Amy set the food on the counter. "And that is that normal around here?"

"Taking care of our neighbors? Yes," Lucas said. "Pretty much everyone knew that Rick's daughter was trying to meet an important deadline. They wanted to help."

She shook her head in disbelief. "Unbelievable."

"Maybe to you." He paused. "By the way, do you have a thermometer in the house?"

Concern for him flickered in her eyes. "Aren't you feeling well?"

"I'm fine," Lucas reassured her, "But John Yoder, the boy who's been our mysterious guest at the antique store, is lying ill in my guest bedroom."

Amy's eyes widened in shock. "Are you kidding me?"

"No," Lucas said. "Sometimes I do kid you, but not about this."

"Go back to him," she said, already moving toward the bathroom. "I'll be right there."

She grabbed the digital thermometer and hurried back to the kitchen while Lucas was still pulling on his coat.

"Let's go." Amy said.

CHAPTER 32

I stood at the bedroom door as Lucas took the boy's temperature and helped him take a few sips of broth he had heated on the stove.

"Your temperature is coming down," he told him. "That is good news. Is there anything else you can think of that you need right now?"

"*Nein.*"

"Then rest. I'll be right outside the door if you need me."

"*Danke.*"

Lucas quietly closed the door behind him, and I took a seat in one of two wooden rocking chairs.

"So, our vagrant is an Amish teenager." I said, softly, in case John could hear through the door. "Isn't that a little odd?"

"It is highly unusual," Lucas said. "Do you feel like having some tea?"

"I do, thank you."

While he filled a teakettle with water and put it on the stove, I glanced around his house. I'd never been inside before and was curious to see how he lived. What I saw was a home that was simple to the extreme. Lucas didn't seem to own much.

There were no pictures on the walls, no family photographs, no knick-knacks of any kind. There were two Amish rockers to sit on in the small living room, and a bench along one wall with a few books stacked on it. The living room and kitchen were all one room. A few plates, cups, and some crockery were placed on the open kitchen shelving. There was a small, round kitchen table with two chairs. Everything was wood, except the walls, which were painted white.

There was a calendar on the wall from the local feed store with a few notations penciled on it. A battery-operated floor lamp illuminated the living room, and a kerosene lamp sat in the middle of the kitchen table. It was growing dark, so while we waited for the kettle to boil, he lit a Coleman lantern that sat on a counter and then rummaged in a drawer for tea bags.

The most colorful thing was an oval rug lying in the middle of the living room floor braided from various shades of blue cloth that matched the curtains in the windows. I had noticed that John's bedroom had been equally plain, except for the purple and black quilt on the bed.

I did not know if such plainness was part of the Amish culture, or if it was simply Lucas's preference.

"Shall I check to see if John would like some tea?" I asked, hoping to be helpful.

"I'll do it." Lucas went into the guest room for a few minutes. When he came back out, the teakettle was boiling. He pulled down two lovely, delicately flowered teacups, which were a surprise to me. I had expected plain white coffee mugs. He filled them with the tea bags and boiling water. Then he added honey without asking. If there was one thing Lucas knew about me, it was how I liked my tea. He'd certainly brought me plenty of cups of it over the past few months.

"His fever seems to have broken." Lucas handed me a steaming teacup, then settled in the other rocking chair. "He's soaked in sweat, but he's sleeping peacefully now. I don't think he'll need a doctor—he certainly didn't want one when I suggested it."

"Did he give you any idea what his story is?" I took a sip. "Why would an Amish boy his age have to live in an old antique store? Doesn't he have any family?"

"He told me his story," Lucas said, "Coming from Pennsylvania to visit cousins who'd moved without telling him. But I don't believe it."

"Why?" I was intrigued.

"The first thing most Amish boys would do in a strange place if they had nowhere to go is to connect with the local Amish community. Most would do that long before they would break into a place of business and face possible interaction with the police. There are plenty of Amish people around here who would take him in without question."

"So, you think something is off about all this?"

"I think there's a lot off with this. I think the boy is in some sort of trouble, but I'm not sure what kind," Lucas said. "But sometimes Amish communities force people out if they don't obey all the rules. In fact—I'm in a bit of trouble with our bishop right now, myself."

"You? That's ridiculous!" I thought he was joking, but then I saw how serious he looked. "What happened, Lucas?"

"I've gotten myself shunned for six months," he said. "The bishop does not approve of the way I've been thinking. He accused me of having a rebellious attitude."

Lucas? Rebellious? The only thing the man ever did was keep the farm running and help people who needed help.

"Your bishop hasn't known many people if he thinks *you* are rebellious."

"It's hard to explain our ways to someone not raised Amish." He stared into his cooling teacup. "The Amish use a very different yardstick to measure one another's behavior. We have many rules that are probably invisible to you."

I was curious. "Like what?"

"Like how many pleats my sisters and nieces can have on their dresses, or how wide a ribbon I can wear on my hat. Whether our suspenders have to be homemade or can be store bought. There are reasons for these rules, but I question the importance of following them."

"And for questioning them, you will be shunned?"

"That and other things. Six months is not a heavy punishment, but it is perhaps a little unfair."

I could tell that he was truly hurt by the bishop's decree. I took a sip of tea and discovered that it had grown cold. I glanced around for a microwave to heat it up. Silly me. This was a non-electric house.

Lucas noticed. "I'll heat that up for you on the stove."

"No need." I gulped down the last of it. "What will being shunned mean for you?"

"My church and family won't be allowed to be part of my life during those six months. I will miss dinners with my sisters."

"You'll have to spend Christmas alone?" I felt a pang of sympathy. "That's only ten days away."

"I have dealt with worse things."

"I won't be having much of a Christmas, either," I admitted. "I thought Mom was coming, but she called and said probably not. Something about a new film, I think."

"Then, I guess we will both be orphans for Christmas," he said.

"I wonder if John has parents that are missing him," I said. "Or if he's an orphan, too."

"No telling what's going on with him until he feels better and trusts us enough to talk," he said. "But when I arrived at the antique store today, he had tried to make his 'room' nicer with some old Christmas decorations. It hurt my heart. He's not much more than a child, and yet he has been eating out of a restaurant's trash bin for months."

"What!"

"You heard me."

"Well, that settles it," I said. "We have a week and a half before Christmas. I don't even want to *look* at a computer again until I get the edits back. Let's get him well, and then I'll fix a nice Christmas Eve meal for us. We might even manage to find a present or two we can put under the tree."

"What tree?"

"The one you are going to find and chop down for me."

"My people do not put up Christmas trees."

"But I do." I said with determination. "So, while I wait for the edits to come back, let's make ourselves a Christmas, Lucas!"

"I don't know…"

"Afraid your bishop will shun you? Seems to me that train has already left the station, my friend. Besides, if that boy has done as much work for me as you say, I owe him a gift or two."

"I will happily go chop down that tree," Lucas said. "It is not forbidden to put a Christmas tree in an *Englisch* person's house."

And so began the happiest ten days of my adult life—preparing for Christmas despite having no blood kin with which to share it.

CHAPTER 33

Within twenty-four hours, the combination of rest, warmth, and nourishing food worked its magic. John regained some of his strength. His cheeks, which had been hollow and pale, now had a faint flush of color, and the world weariness in his eyes lifted.

Lucas could see the boy's spirit reviving, and it was a relief to watch. The frail, feverish teenager he'd found huddled in Rick's store was slowly transforming into someone ready to engage with the world around him.

Amy's enthusiasm for creating a Christmas for the three of them was infectious. She threw herself into the preparations with a child-like joy that Lucas found both surprising and heartwarming. She bustled about, humming Christmas carols as she decorated the living room with strings of paper garlands and handmade ornaments she purchased in town.

It wasn't extravagant, but the effort and care she put into it made Rick's house feel almost holy. Lucas hadn't celebrated Christmas with much enthusiasm since his wife had died, but watching Amy, he felt a spark of holiday magic flicker back to life.

Although John clung stubbornly to his story of being an Amish boy from Pennsylvania, it became increasingly clear to Lucas that something about his story wasn't adding up. When Amy offered to drive the boy back home if he wanted to go, his hesitation was immediate and profound. He did not want to leave.

"I'd rather finish cleaning and organizing the antique store before I go, if you don't mind," he'd said hastily, a note of desperation in his voice. "I like to finish a job once I start."

Lucas exchanged a glance with Amy, silently acknowledging that John's story had more holes than a piece of Sugarcreek's award-winning Swiss cheese, but neither of them pressed him. Instead, they let him be, hoping that with time and trust, he would trust them enough to tell the truth.

John had only the clothes on his back, and they needed laundered badly. He didn't weigh as much as Lucas, but they were about the same height, so with the addition of a belt and suspenders, and rolling up his shirt sleeves, he had clean clothes to wear.

Lucas chose not to embarrass the boy by speaking to him in Pennsylvania Deutsch anymore. He had tried once or twice, but it soon became clear that John had picked up only a few phrases here and there, just enough to get by but not enough to pass as fluent. Lucas decided it was best to let it go, pretending not to notice the boy's lack of understanding. He didn't want to confront him yet with what he suspected.

As the days passed, Amy seemed full of mysterious plans, making several trips to town. Lucas was reasonably sure her plans involved gifts of some kind, though she was being cagey about the details. That was fine by him. It wasn't long before he, too, was caught up in the holiday preparations. He and John had several long talks about what they might do for Amy.

"If I had some acrylic paints," John said one evening, his voice thoughtful, "I think I might make something she'd like. My high school art teacher said I was pretty good."

Lucas paused at that, realizing the boy had made another slip. Amish teenagers didn't go to high school. John mentioning one was a glaring inconsistency in his story. Lucas said nothing, letting it slide. The boy clearly had his reasons for keeping his past a secret, and Lucas wasn't about to force his hand unless it became necessary.

Instead, Lucas hitched up the buggy the next day, and they drove to what the locals called the "Amish Walmart," a large, locally owned mercantile store that sold just about everything under the sun. Not only did he purchase paint for John, but he also bought him a new pair of boots, which he badly needed. The tennis shoes John had been wearing—his only footwear—were falling apart and completely unsuited for winter. The look of quiet gratitude in John's eyes when Lucas handed him the boots was worth every penny.

"May I clean your workshop to pay you back?" John asked as he got back into Lucas's buggy, clutching the paint and boots like they were treasures.

"If you want to," Lucas said, his tone light. "When you feel strong enough."

"I feel strong enough," John insisted. "And I want to."

Nothing about the arrangement was ideal, but Lucas found himself grateful for the boy's company. The cheerful presence of John was a balm for the loneliness that had crept in during these early days of his six-month shunning.

He spent a great deal of time praying that John would eventually trust him enough to tell the truth. The boy had been through something bad—Lucas could sense it—but whatever it was, he wasn't ready to share it yet.

In the meantime, Lucas began crafting a wooden jewelry box for Amy. His people wore no jewelry, but she had a few earrings and a necklace or two he'd noticed. He spent hours in his workshop, sanding and shaping the wood, carefully choosing each piece so that the finished product would be something beautiful. John, true to his word, spent the time cleaning and organizing the workshop, making it easier for Lucas to work. Then he set up a makeshift easel and started to paint.

CHAPTER 34

I was sitting at the kitchen table, scribbling down a last-minute grocery list for our little Christmas party tomorrow evening, when my cell phone rang. My heart skipped a beat when I saw the caller ID. It was from Ezekiel.

I hadn't heard from him since I sent the manuscript, and I couldn't help but feel a twinge of anxiety as I answered the call. Trying to keep my voice from shaking, I said hello, praying this wasn't the call where he told me he hated everything I'd written.

"You sound funny," Ezekiel's deep voice rumbled through the line, a hint of concern lacing his words. "Why?"

"Oh, nothing," I replied, trying to keep the worry out of my voice. "Just getting ready for Christmas."

"You got a lot of people coming in?" he asked, sounding wistful.

"Nope," I said, glancing at the sparse decorations around the kitchen. "It's just me, my Amish farm manager, and a stray boy who's staying here. We're having a good dinner, though. Turkey, cranberry sauce, stuffing, you name it."

"I figured you'd be having some big family thing."

"Sorry. Not happening." I felt a pang of sadness. Christmas had always felt lonely for me, with Mom always jetting off somewhere, although Rick had tried to make it special when he'd lived with us. "What about you? What are you doing?"

"I'm letting my people off for Christmas," E.C. said, his voice softening. "They need to be with their families."

"I'm sure they appreciate that, but how are you celebrating? Any family coming in?"

"Nah." There was a touch of studied nonchalance in his voice that didn't fool me. "I don't really have any family anymore. I'll sleep in, watch some movies, see what restaurants might be open."

There was something about the way he said it that made me pause. I'd known enough celebrities to understand that, despite all the adoring fans and the constant spotlight, it could sometimes be a very lonely life. I hesitated, biting my lip as I weighed my next words.

"I know it's a long way to come," I began, "but if you'd like to have Christmas dinner here with us tomorrow night, there's plenty of room at my table."

There was a long pause on the other end of the line, so long that I wondered if I'd overstepped. But then I heard E.C. clear his throat, and when he spoke again, there was a warmth in his voice that hadn't been there before.

"I just bought myself a new car and I'm back home in Detroit right now. Not that far to drive." His tone was lighter, almost playful. "Wouldn't mind seeing that farm of yours. Got nothing else to do."

I smiled, feeling a wave of relief and something else—something that felt a lot like pure happiness—wash over me. "We'd love to have you. Dinner is at six tomorrow night. I'll set an extra plate. I'll text you the address. Just promise you'll be careful on these snowy roads."

"Don't worry about me, girl," he said. "I'll be fine."

My mind was already racing with thoughts of what I could add to the menu to make it special. "I'm really glad you're coming, Ezekiel."

"Me too," he said, and I could hear genuine gratitude in his voice. "See you tomorrow."

After I hung up, I sat there for a moment, the phone still in my hand. I hadn't expected him to say yes, hadn't expected him to make the trip all the way to this snowy little corner of Ohio. But he was coming, and the thought made me happy.

With renewed energy, I picked up my grocery list again, adding a few more items I thought he'd like, including that special brand of water he liked. This Christmas was turning out to be very different from what I had planned, and I was good with that.

Then I realized he hadn't mentioned the book at all, even though he'd had it in his possession for several days.

CHAPTER 35

I was pulling pots and pans out of the cabinets for all the side dishes I intended to cook today. The turkey was baking in the oven. I was humming Christmas carols and feeling pleasantly domestic, when I heard the crunch of tires on the gravel driveway. I glanced out the window and saw a sleek car pulling in. Before I even had time to deal with my dismay, my mother, Desireé, burst through the kitchen door.

Seriously? My first reaction was annoyance—why couldn't she just be like other moms with a normal schedule? I'd have loved it if we could have cooked dinner together. Christmas carols playing in the background while we decorated cookies came to mind.

Then I realized an attitude shift was in order. At least she'd made the effort to come! I even had plenty of food to go around.

"Hello, darling! Merry Christmas!" she sang out, her voice bright and tinkly as Christmas bells. She'd chosen white wool slacks, white leather boots, a red sweater, and a forest green scarf. And to top it all off—literally—she wore blinking antlers on her head. Of course she did.

This was typical Desireé. Socially, she didn't like being held to a schedule, and her travel plans were as whimsical as her fashion choices.

"What a pleasant surprise, Mother," I said, meaning it. Desiree wasn't like other moms, but I loved her the best I knew how, and in her way, she loved me. I knew she had gone to a lot of trouble to surprise me. It would have been nice had she let me know, but oh well. "I didn't know you were coming for Christmas."

"Oh, I'm not staying," she announced, waving a perfectly manicured hand as if to brush away the very idea. "I just wanted to stop in for a few minutes, say hi, and remind you that you are not a farmer." She flashed me a knowing smile. "You can't even keep a houseplant alive, remember?"

She wasn't wrong. House plants didn't last long in my apartment—never had.

"Thank goodness you don't have any children," she continued, her voice dripping with faux concern. "With your record with houseplants, a child would never survive."

It was Christmas. I chose not to point out that surviving my mother's particular style of parenting hadn't been all that easy, either.

"Thank you for pointing that out, Mother," I said drily. "To what do I owe this visit?"

"I brought you a gift."

"A Christmas gift?" For a moment, I felt a small bubble of excitement.

"You could call it that." Desireé's tone shifted to one of earnest concern. "You realize that it's unthinkable for you to continue to bury yourself way out here in the boonies. Right?"

"But…" I started to protest. She held up a hand to stop me.

"I've been looking up real estate prices in Tuscarawas County. Two hundred acres plus this house and the little house where that Amish farmer lives would bring in more than enough to buy us an excellent condo in Manhattan with plenty of room, and money left over.

Did she say "us?"

I barely suppressed a laugh. It was I who paid for my apartment, not "us." My mother stopped by for a few days each year, like a bird resting up after a long flight. Then once she'd recuperated, off she'd go, leaving the apartment a jumbled nest of discarded clothes, jewelry, and magazines.

Experience had taught me that Desireé could sometimes be certifiably selfish, but I was still shocked that practically the first thing out of her mouth after hearing about Rick's funeral had been speculation over what my inheritance might be worth.

"Don't you care that Rick's gone at all?" I asked.

"Of course I care," she said, her tone dismissive. "It's quite tragic. But we must be practical. Rick was always tight with his money. It's one reason I divorced him. He probably still has quite a pile lying about."

"He doesn't," I told her. "There was barely enough money in the bank to bury him. From what I've learned, he spent most of what he made helping people he cared about. Rick was a good man. Even better than I realized when I was a child."

"Of course, he was a good man, darling." Desiree had grown bored. "I have never married a bad one."

"How long can you stay, Mom?" I asked politely, trying to change the subject and curb the discomfort gnawing at my insides. Her pacing back and forth was worrying me.

"I can't stay long. I fly back out this evening."

"Where to this time?" I asked.

"Granada. Philippe, my new friend, is a hotelier I met in France. He invited me to spend Christmas in his newest acquisition. You know how much I love the Caribbean in winter."

"Not really," I muttered under my breath. Wherever she was going next was always her 'favorite.'

"In fact," Desireé said brightly. "I brought him along with me. He's been trying to find just the right location to build one of his hotels right here in America. I told him about the tourism here and about your lovely piece of property. I showed him photos I took the last time I was here, and he is thinking about making you an offer. A very generous offer."

"What?" I couldn't believe what I was hearing.

"Surprise!" Desireé threw up her arms in celebration. "Merry Christmas! This is the Christmas present I was telling you about!"

"But I don't want to sell. You know this."

"You need to hear what his company will offer before you decide."

"I don't care, Mother," I said, my frustration bubbling to the surface. "I will not force a big, ugly hotel on my neighbors."

"Then what are you going to do with it?" she demanded.

"Enjoy it!" I snapped, feeling cornered. "Live in it. Use it as a personal writing retreat. Grow things. I hate to break it to you, Mother, but I'm seriously thinking about moving here permanently."

"It's a little too late to tell me you want to keep the place," she said, sounding miffed. "Philippe is outside looking over our property right now."

I rushed to the window. Sure enough, a dapper little man was wandering around outside, taking pictures, and talking on the phone. Where was Lucas? I looked around frantically. I did not want him to see or hear any of this.

"How could you?" I asked, seething at her presumption.

"What? What did I do?" she said, feigning innocence.

"I will not sell my land!"

"I don't think you know what's best for you," Desireé said. "Burying yourself away in this place! I raised you better than that. How will you ever find a man—at least a man who doesn't wear suspenders and have dirt under his fingernails?"

"I'll be fine, Mother." I struggled to keep my voice steady. "I can take care of myself with or without a man. I have for years."

At that moment, Phillippe knocked on the door, and my mother let him in. Her voice became all kittenish as she took his hat and coat and introduced us.

"Well?" she said. "What do you think?"

"You were right, *mon amour*, it is perfect," Philippe said, then he turned his attention to me. "Your mother tells me you do not want to sell?"

"That's right."

"Maybe I can change your mind." He wrote something on the back of a business card and handed it to me. I looked at it and caught my breath.

"I am so sorry, but we must run. My plane is waiting." Philippe handed me an elegant business card. "It is wonderful to meet Desireé's beautiful daughter."

Right.

After giving air kisses and a quick hug, Desireé departed, leaving me standing there with my mind racing. I was torn between shock and disbelief.

As they drove away, my mother rolled down the window and called out, "Merry Christmas, darling. You can thank me later!"

I watched them disappear down the driveway, my mind reeling.

CHAPTER 36

Lucas carefully screwed the tiny hinge in place. The jewelry box was finished, and it wasn't just any jewelry box. He'd poured his skill into it, and it was beautiful.

The box had two small drawers, each one lined with soft velvet he had carefully cut and fit. Each had its own tiny, silver knob he had been delighted to find at Keim Lumber, nearby in Charm. He had designed a secret compartment too, hidden so cleverly that even someone examining it closely might miss it.

The wood he'd chosen was special. It was well-seasoned wild cherry, its rich, reddish-brown hues warm and inviting. He had been saving that wood for the right project, and this was the right one.

He ran his hands over the smooth surface, feeling the grain beneath his fingers. The cherry wood had a deep luster, glowing softly in the light of his workshop. He had spent hours sanding, polishing and perfecting every detail, ensuring that the box was as beautiful as it was functional.

He imagined Amy opening the gift, her eyes lighting up with surprise and delight. That thought alone made him smile.

Lucas stepped back to admire his work, but his satisfaction was marred by an anxiety that surprised him. He wanted this gift to be something she cherished, something that made her think of him whenever she opened it.

Her presence was becoming too important to him. He hadn't expected this. The ramifications were too great to even think about. And yet he awoke every morning a little happier because of her, and he often went to bed chuckling about something she'd done or said. It was not wrong, regardless of what Bishop Yoder said, but it was troubling.

Lucas carefully wiped away the last traces of sawdust. He wrapped the jewelry box in a soft cloth and left it on his workshop bench, ready to be wrapped for Christmas.

Amy was Rick's daughter, his employer, and his friend. There was nothing wrong with making it his Christmas gift to her.

CHAPTER 37

By the time Christmas evening rolled around, I was worn out and my feet ached from standing all day. But the delicious scent of turkey, sage stuffing, and gravy wafting through the kitchen made it worth all the effort.

I had spent the entire day juggling pots and pans in the kitchen while simultaneously fielding call after call from my mother. It was unfortunate that some airlines had started allowing passengers to make calls while in flight. Desireé had grown bored, and phoning me became her favorite way to pass the time.

"You've really landed on your feet, Amy. Don't blow it," she said during her latest call, her voice filled with a mix of annoyance and grudging admiration. "I can't believe you're even hesitating."

I rubbed my temples, trying to stave off the headache that had been building all day. "I don't want to sell, Mom. I love it here, and my neighbors would hate me for doing something like that."

"No, they won't," Desireé replied with her usual dismissiveness. "They'll get jobs at the hotel and be grateful for them."

"You don't understand. It would kill Lucas to see the land used like that. He has become a good friend. I could never do that to him."

"Friends are a dime a dozen when you're young and rich," she said. "But this might be your only chance to secure a truly comfortable future for yourself. I don't want you to have to work as hard as I have, sweetheart."

I sighed, the weight of her words pressing down on me. "I'm finishing Christmas Eve dinner, Mom. I can't talk anymore. Be safe and let me know where you are from time to time. Please tell Philippe that I'm not interested."

"I refuse to tell him that!" she snapped, her frustration showing. "Amy, listen to me—"

But I'd had enough. I hung up, cutting off her words mid-sentence. As I sat the phone down on the counter, I could still hear Lucas's voice echoing in my mind, steady and sure: "This is fertile land, Amy. They aren't making any more of it. It will sustain life if you treat it well."

I closed my eyes, letting his words sink in, trying to drown out the lingering doubts that my mother had planted. The temptation of the offer was there, lingering like an ugly shadow in the back of my mind. The amount of money Philippe had proposed was staggering. I could have the freedom to write anything I wanted or nothing at all. I could travel anywhere, do anything, without the pressure of needing to worry about a job.

But what would I give up in exchange? The peace and beauty of this valley, the kindness of the neighbors who had embraced and supported me, and the friendship of a man who had grown to mean more to me than I'd ever expected. Could I really trade all of that for a pile of money, no matter how large?

I opened my eyes and looked around the kitchen. The warmth of the oven, the smell of food cooking, the small decorations I'd put up— I wanted to hug this feeling to my heart and never let go.

I knew, deep down, that I simply couldn't go through with it, no matter how hard my mother pushed. The money wasn't worth the cost. And as much as Desiree argued, as much as she tried to convince me otherwise, this was my decision. I was staying, and that was the end of the discussion.

I walked over to the oven and checked on the food, feeling a sense of resolve settle over me. I'd made my choice, and it was absolutely the right one.

CHAPTER 38

J ust as I was lighting the candles and fussing over the decorations at the last minute, I heard a car coming down the driveway. At least I thought it was a car. It sounded different. The motor didn't just run; it purred, smooth and rich. Curious, I glanced outside and did a double take when I saw a black Porsche, all tricked out with cobalt blue trim. Not the kind of vehicle you'd expect to see in the middle of Amish country.

I opened the door, and there was E.C. himself, dreadlocks cascading down his back, standing on my porch in a full-length faux white fur coat that screamed "celebrity." In his hands, he held a huge sparkly basket of fancy fruit. It would be hard to look more out of place than he did at that moment, and yet my heart leaped with joy!

"Hey there, girl. Merry Christmas." He flashed that trademark grin of his.

"Merry Christmas, Ezekiel," I replied. "Gorgeous car!"

"Yeah," he said. "I get to buy myself nice toys these days." He handed me the giant fruit basket. "Lame, I know, but it was the only thing I could find on short notice."

"I love fruit." I took the basket from him as he stepped into the kitchen. "Especially in the middle of the winter."

I noticed he also had a leather messenger bag slung over his shoulder. Wasting no time, he opened it, pulled out a printed copy of my manuscript, and slapped it on the kitchen counter.

"*Songs from the Beat of My Brother's Heart?* That's the title you chose?"

"We can change it."

He stared at me for what felt like an eternity, his face unreadable. My mind raced—had I offended him? Did he hate the book? The silence stretched out too long. I held my breath, waiting for him to say something, anything.

Finally, he gave a slow nod. "You did it, girl. I don't know how you managed, but you nailed it. I couldn't have told it any better."

The relief that washed over me was so intense, I had to hold back tears. The enormous weight I'd been carrying suddenly lifted off my shoulders, and I knew that whatever changes my editor might suggest later would be easy after this moment.

"I'm thrilled you're happy with it," I said.

"It's going to be a bestseller." A hint of pride was in his voice. "Might even inspire a person or two."

"Wouldn't that be something?" I said.

As we stood there, caught up in the moment, Lucas and John let themselves in. They were dressed alike. Black broadfall pants with suspenders, white collarless shirts, and black hats. It looked like they might have also given each other haircuts for the occasion.

"Let me introduce you to my friends." I gestured for them to join us.

Lucas acted like he encountered a six-foot-tall black man with dreadlocks and a full-length white faux fur coat every day of his life. But John? John was vibrating with excitement. His eyes went wide, like he couldn't believe what he was seeing.

"E.C.?" John said with awe. "Is that really you?"

"It was me the last time I checked." Ezekiel extended a hand.

"I've listened to all your albums over and over.," John said. "Every word."

"Amish kids like rap?" E.C. asked, genuinely interested. "I had no idea."

John suddenly looked worried. I exchanged a glance with Lucas, who raised an eyebrow but didn't say anything.

"I don't know about other Amish kids," John finally said. "But I certainly do!"

"If everyone's hungry, dinner's ready," I said. "I just need to set all the food out."

"I'll help," Lucas offered, and we headed toward the kitchen.

"John," I said, turning back, "do you mind keeping Ezekiel company while we get things ready?"

"Sure!" he replied. "I have so many questions."

Once we were alone in the kitchen, I turned to Lucas, my curiosity getting the better of me. "Seriously? Do Amish kids listen to rap?"

"Probably more than you'd think," he said. "Kids are kids. They're going to find a way to listen to what the others are, no matter where they come from."

"I guess you're right." We fell into a comfortable rhythm, setting out the dinner and making certain everything was just right.

"I had no idea you could cook like this," Lucas said. "Did your mother teach you?"

"Desiree?" I laughed. "No. She hired a woman named Trudy to be our housekeeper and cook. One of the smartest things Mom ever did."

"Sounds interesting." Lucas put the festive red napkins I'd bought beside each plate. "Tell me about it."

"Trudy was from some backwoods place in Kentucky and had come to Hollywood to become a star. Mom had met her on a set somewhere. You wouldn't believe the people who show up in L.A. from tiny towns hoping to make a name for themselves. Trudy wasn't much of an actress, but she could cook."

"Where does this go?" Lucas asked, holding a heaping platter of biscuits.

"On the side table beside the butter," I said.

"Keep telling me how you learned to cook," Lucas said.

"Trudy came into our life when I was a teenager. She was only in her twenties, but she'd grown up on a hardscrabble farm and knew how to do things—odd things for L.A.— like how to fix a tractor or trap a rabbit. Desiree was on location in Alaska, which meant Trudy and I were on our own together."

"That must have felt strange."

"Not entirely. I was used to Mom being gone a lot, but I didn't enjoy being left with a hired stranger. I was busy feeling sorry for myself at the time, and Trudy grew tired of it. She told me to get my lazy bottom off the couch and take out the trash. I told her she wasn't the boss of me, and then I made a crack about it being impossible to find good help these days."

"What happened after that?" Lucas had stopped paying attention to anything except the story.

"Trudy spent the next half-hour letting me know who was boss. It got pretty loud, but she made her point, and I took out the trash. After that, she taught me how to cook for myself so she wouldn't have to. By the time Mom got home, we'd become good friends."

"Whatever happened to Trudy?" he asked.

"Last I heard, she'd gotten interested in politics and was running for mayor of her hometown."

CHAPTER 39

As Lucas and I worked together and Ezekiel and John talked, I felt a sense of contentment wash over me. The feast I had cooked for our Christmas Eve meal turned out as well as I'd hoped. The roasted turkey was perfect, the potatoes fluffy; the dressing was deliciously savory, and the veggies were perfectly steamed. The whole spread looked and smelled like a scene from a holiday movie, and I allowed myself to bask in it.

Everyone seemed to be having a great time, which made all the preparations today while dealing with my mother's constant calls worth it.

I sat back and enjoyed John's boundless enthusiasm as he peppered E.C. with questions about his lyrics. Ezekiel seemed to enjoy getting to dive deep into his work with someone who appreciated it so much.

Then everything went wrong.

John reached across the table for a bowl of glazed carrots, and as he did, the sleeve of his shirt rode up. I wouldn't have noticed anything unusual, but Ezekiel's eyes suddenly narrowed. His hand shot out, and he grabbed John's wrist with a swiftness that startled all of us, then he jerked John's sleeve up.

The room fell into silence, the laughter and easy conversation evaporated.

E.C. turned John's wrist over, exposing the underside. There, on the boy's skin, was a small tattoo that I had not noticed. It was an intricate design, no bigger than a quarter, but it seemed to have great significance for Ezekiel.

"Tell me I'm not seeing what I think I see!" Ezekiel stared at the tattoo; his voice was thick with disbelief.

John's face drained of color. He tried to pull his arm back, but E.C. held it tight.

"I'm not that person anymore!" John said. "I never was."

I looked back and forth between them, lost.

"I don't understand," I said.

"I don't either," Lucas added.

E.C. didn't look at us. He didn't take his eyes off John.

"Tell them," E.C. said.

"They won't understand," John muttered, his eyes filled with shame.

"These are good people who have taken you in," E.C. said, finally letting go of John's arm. "They deserve to know what you are. Tell them."

"I can't," John whispered.

The easy camaraderie we had been enjoying was gone. No one so much as lifted a fork. We all just sat there, waiting. The tension in the room felt suffocating.

"Tell them," E.C. repeated, his voice hard. "Or I will."

But John remained silent, his eyes cast down, his body tense with the weight of whatever secret he was keeping.

"This is no Amish kid you've taken in," E.C. said. "He's a member of the most vicious gang in Detroit. They would kill their own grandmother if their leader told them to. It was the same gang that killed my brother."

I felt the blood drain from my face. "Is this true?" I asked John.

176

John looked at E.C. with a mix of fear and sorrow. "I used to hang out with them," he admitted. "Then I listened to the album you dedicated to Michael. I listened to it over and over. It helped clear my mind. I started to think for myself. It made me realize things could be different and should be different."

"I hurt nobody!" He turned to face me, his eyes pleading for understanding. "I swear, I hurt nobody! I wanted to get out, but there's no way to leave that group and survive. They track you down. They have a saying, 'Blood in, blood out.' That means when you join, you join for life. "

I felt a chill run down my spine. "Why did you pretend to be Amish?" I asked, trying to make sense of it all.

"I saw an old movie—the one where the cop hides out from the bad guys by staying with some Amish people," he explained. "I had no money and no friends who would take me in and hide me. I thought pretending to be Amish might be one way to disappear."

"But why move into Rick's store?" Lucas sounded deeply concerned.

"The first time I walked into the store, Rick was there," he said. "I was looking for something to steal so I could sell it and buy some food. He saw me and knew what I was doing. Instead of calling the cops, he had a pizza delivered to the store. He fed me and talked with me. Found out what I was trying to do. He told me to find myself a place to sleep. Said I could be his 'night watchman.' He even gave me some money. Then one day, he didn't come back, and I didn't know what to do. Except to stay hidden as long as possible."

"Are you still in danger?" I asked, my heart heavy with worry.

"He's in danger as long as he lives." E.C. answered for him. "It's a matter of honor for those young thugs."

John's face filled with anguish. "I'm sorry I lied and fooled all of you into thinking I was Amish," he said, his voice barely above a whisper. "But I didn't know what else to do."

"You didn't fool me," Lucas said.

John looked up, surprised. "How did you know?"

"So many things," Lucas said. "But the first was your clothes."

"My clothes?"

"You were wearing Old Order Amish pants, New Order Amish suspenders, a store-bought button-down shirt, and a Swartzentruber hat—with someone else's name written inside the brim," Lucas said. "I figured you'd found some Amish clothing at one of our thrift stores, but I couldn't figure out why you'd want to."

John looked stunned. "You didn't say anything."

"Didn't need to," Lucas replied gently. "I figured you were probably in trouble. I didn't know why, but I wanted to help. I waited until you trusted me enough to tell me what was going on."

At that moment, my cell phone buzzed, cutting through the heavy silence. I glanced at it and saw my mother's name flashing on the screen. Again. Of all times. I shut it off. It rang again.

"Excuse me," I said, rising from the table. "I'll take this out on the porch."

I stepped outside into the cold night air, my head spinning from everything that had just happened. I didn't want to answer the call, but I knew Desiree would just keep dialing until I did. I clicked it on speakerphone so I wouldn't have to press it against my ear, which was feeling a little raw from all her incessant calls today.

"Hello, darling," Desireé's voice trilled as soon as I answered. "Are you ready for another Christmas present?"

"Probably not," I replied, trying to keep the irritation out of my voice.

She ignored me. "Philippe did some research, and he agrees that the hotel they're going to build on your property needs to look more rustic."

"Mom…" I started, but she cut me off.

"Oh, and he thinks they can up the price even more. You'll be such a rich woman, sweetheart. Won't that be fun?"

I heard a noise behind me and turned to see Lucas standing in the open door. His eyes were filled with hurt. He didn't say a word, just walked past me toward the barn. A moment later, I heard horse's hooves as he galloped away from the house.

I stood there, the phone still in my hand, watching him disappear into the night. What had he heard? What had he thought? What did he think of me? Had I just lost what I was beginning to suspect was the best friend I'd ever had?

CHAPTER 40

L ucas didn't come back. Except for the hum of conversation between Ezekiel and John, the house felt empty.

"Why did Lucas leave?" John asked, when he stopped talking long enough to notice.

"I don't know," I said. "He overheard me talking to Mom about someone who wants to buy the farm. I will not sell it, but Lucas doesn't know that. I think it upset him."

"You oughta go after him and let him know," Ezekiel said, breaking through my thoughts. "Go see if you can find him. John and I will clean up."

"Thank you, but where would I look? He could be anywhere."

"No, he couldn't," John chimed in. "He's being shunned. He can't go to anyone in his church or to his family. There're no restaurants open tonight in Sugarcreek, but he has a key to the antique store. It's heated there, and he can be alone."

"I'll go check," I said, feeling a glimmer of hope. "That's a great suggestion."

"Yeah, and when you find him, tell him you ain't gonna sell this place," Ezekiel added, his voice firm. "No matter how much they offer you."

"Most people would jump at it," I said. "But even the thought of selling this place sickens me."

"Listen to me," Ezekiel said. "That little kid you been writing a book about? He survived by learning how to read people real good and real fast. Forget your crazy-as-a-bat mama. That Lucas is a good man. You better hold on to him." E.C.'s voice was dead serious.

"He's my farm manager." I tried to brush off the implications. "A friend. Nothing else."

"Yeah, yeah, and I'm Santa Claus," E.C. shot back, rolling his eyes. "He wants you for his lady, only he don't know it yet."

"Are you serious?"

"E.C. is right," John added. "Lucas has been working on a really nice Christmas present for you every minute he has to spare. A man doesn't do that for someone he doesn't care about."

"Go after him," Ezekiel urged. "Patch things up. Me and my man, John, will be here when you get back."

"Thank you," I said, feeling a rush of gratitude as I grabbed my coat and headed out the door.

A few minutes later, I drove through downtown Sugarcreek, my heart pounding as I spotted Lucas's horse tied to a hitching post behind the antique store. Relief flooded through me at finding him so easily.

Lucas hadn't bothered to lock the door. I let myself in, and found him sitting on one of the couches, staring into a cold fireplace. He didn't turn around when I entered the room, but I could sense the weight of his thoughts, the turmoil that must be running through his mind.

"I'm sorry you had to hear that conversation between me and my mom," I said, my voice barely more than a whisper. "If you'd stayed until our conversation was over, you would have heard me once again, refusing to sell."

"It's okay," Lucas's voice was flat, devoid of the warmth I'd come to expect from him. "The property belongs to you. You can do whatever you want with it. I can't keep worrying about it."

His words cut because I could hear the terrible resignation in them.

"But I'm not going to sell," I said. "I tried to tell Mom and her friend that from the beginning, but Mom sort of rolls all over people when she gets an idea. It's like she forgets how to listen."

"She just wants the best for you," Lucas said.

"What if I don't agree with her about what's best for me?" I asked.

"You need to move back to the city and sell the farm to developers. Or let it grow into weeds." Lucas shook his head. "I don't care. I'm tired. I cannot spend my life waiting and wondering. Will Amy sell? Won't she? Maybe she'll sell next year. Maybe the year after. I would rather start all over than live like this."

His words stung, but I knew he was speaking the truth. He needed something solid to hold on to, something certain in a world that was anything but.

"I was going to wait until tomorrow to give you your Christmas present." I sat down beside him and pulled out an envelope from my purse. "But I think now is a better time."

He showed no enthusiasm as he opened it, but as he glanced at the papers inside, I saw his expression change. He sat up straight and focused on the words.

"A partnership?" Disbelief and happiness warred in his voice.

"An equal one," I said. "I've given it a lot of thought. It's fair to us both. I went to see Cassie Reynolds last week and had her draw up the papers. You told me once that you've often done business based on a handshake. Your business philosophy is that if you say you'll do something, you just do it—but Lucas, that leaves you at the mercy of others. I might be a writer, but that doesn't mean I'm stupid about business and you shouldn't allow yourself to be."

He looked at the papers again, his eyes narrowing as he read more carefully. "Rick's Organic Acres? Rick never named the place."

"That name is non-negotiable," I said. "The food we will grow is going to be Rick's legacy to the people of this community."

"A partnership," Lucas repeated, staring at the papers as if he couldn't quite believe what he was seeing.

"You'll find the terms fair," I said, trying to sound confident. "I'm willing to work out extra details. I think it would be a shame for you to walk away from all you've done. I might not understand everything you do, but I want to support what you are trying to accomplish. I might even help you sometimes when I'm not writing. At least I'd like to try."

"Sometimes," Lucas reached for my hand, his touch gentle but firm, "I wish you were an Amish woman."

"And sometimes…" I felt myself relax, the warmth of his hand grounding me. "I wish you were not an Amish man."

"But I am Amish, and you are not," he said, his voice softening as he looked into my eyes. "And here we are."

"Yes, here we are," I echoed, feeling a bittersweet pang in my heart. I wished we could stay like this forever—sitting close, holding hands, wrapped in the warmth of each other's company. I had seldom felt such a profound sense of safety and peace.

"I will be a good business partner for you," Lucas said, his voice steady and sincere. "But I can be nothing else."

"I understand," I said, though my heart ached a little at the truth of his words. "And I will be a good business partner for you, too. For what it's worth, I'm going to sublet my apartment in Manhattan and live here full time."

"You are staying in Sugarcreek?" he asked, surprise flickering in his eyes.

"I think it would be foolish not to," I replied.

He thought about that for a moment and then chuckled, the sound low and comforting.

"What are you laughing about?" I asked.

"Bishop Yoder will not be happy," he said, shaking his head with a wry smile. "But then, he is not happy about much."

When we returned to the house, Ezekiel and John were practicing rap lyrics together, their voices filling the room with energy.

"You guys patch things up?" E.C. asked, glancing over at us with a knowing look.

"We did," Lucas said, his voice relaxed. "How are things here?"

"John thinks he might like to go back to New York with me early tomorrow," E.C. said, his tone casual. "I have a solid security team. He'll be safe with me, and I can find uses for a smart kid like him. You okay with that?"

"If it is okay with John, it is okay with me," Lucas said. "I do not think there is much future for John in continuing to pretend to be an Amish man."

"I guess we need to open gifts tonight, then," I said, feeling a warm anticipation. "I've already given Lucas his."

"It is a partnership," Lucas said, his voice pleased. "Drawn up by a lawyer, so she cannot change her mind."

"Let me see that," E.C. said, his interest piqued. "I know my way around contracts."

"I'm sure it is fine," Lucas said, but E.C. was already reading through the papers with a critical eye.

"Shhh. I'm reading," E.C. said, his tone serious as he focused on the contract.

We waited in silence as he perused the agreement, the room filled with a quiet tension.

"You better sign this quick, man," E.C. finally said, handing Lucas a pen. "This lady is giving you a sweet deal."

Lucas didn't hesitate. He signed the papers.

"Your gift is under the tree," I said to John, eager to see his reaction.

John pulled out a brightly wrapped box and opened it, his eyes widening as he saw the two complete sets of new, warm and stylish *Englisch* clothes inside.

"Real clothes!" John looked up at me with a sheepish grin. "A belt! Thank you! I really don't like wearing suspenders!"

Lucas handed me a large, square package wrapped in brown burlap in a crate, his eyes shining with anticipation.

"And what is this?" I asked, carefully unfolding the wrapping.

"I hope you will like it," Lucas said, with quiet pride.

Inside was an exquisitely handmade jewelry box, its craftsmanship flawless and the design simple yet elegant.

"It is for your jewelry, or whatever you wish to use it for," Lucas said. "It also has a secret compartment."

"I need me one of them things," E.C. said, eyeing the box with appreciation. "I got a lot of jewelry."

"Thank you, Lucas," I said, my voice soft with gratitude. "I love it."

"I can hardly wait to give you mine," John said, handing me a square, flat package wrapped in festive paper. "It's for both you and Lucas."

I carefully unwrapped the gift and gasped when I saw what was inside. It was a vibrant painting of the farm, the colors rich and full of life. Splashes of yellow and gold captured the warmth of fall, while a red and orange sun was just beginning to peek over the horizon.

At the bottom right corner was the name Cameron Blake and the date.

"Your name is Cameron?" I asked, surprised by the revelation.

"Yeah," he said, quietly. "I picked my Amish name off the internet."

"I will treasure this forever," I said, my heart swelling with emotion. "And always know that you have a home here, Cameron."

"And a job," Lucas added with a warm smile. "We can always use a good worker around here."

"E.C." I said, turning to him, "I'm sorry, but I didn't know you were coming in time to find a gift for you."

"Seriously, girl?" E.C. held up the manuscript, his grin wide. "Best present I ever got."

"That means more than you know." I said. "Now, Lucas, if you and Cameron don't mind hanging this beautiful painting over the fireplace mantle in my office, I have some pie and ice cream that needs our attention."

As I went to dish out their dessert, my mind was filled to overflowing with the Christmas gift Rick had given me—the gift of this place, this life. I wondered if he'd had any inkling about how much it would come to mean to me, how much it would change my life for the better. Knowing Rick Downey, he had thought about all those episodes we had watched together of *Little House on the Prairie* and remembered how badly I had once wanted to be Laura.

"Merry Christmas, Rick," I whispered as I sliced the pie, my heart full of gratitude. "You were the best father a little girl could have."

AUTHOR'S NOTE

Welcome to Sugarcreek, Ohio, where the clip-clop of horse hooves mingles with the hum of modern life, and where mysteries don't always involve murder, but are no less intriguing. As a lover of cozy mysteries myself, I've often wondered why our genre seems to require a body count. After all, life's most compelling mysteries often revolve around the secrets we keep, the treasures we hide, and the stories behind everyday objects.

When I created Rick's Attic—the three-story antique store at the heart of this series—I imagined a place where each item on its dusty shelves might hold a story waiting to be discovered. As a former Sotheby's appraiser, Rick Downey had an eye for the extraordinary hiding in plain sight. Now his stepdaughter Amy, along with her Amish farm manager Lucas, will uncover these stories one by one, proving that in a small town like Sugarcreek, the most fascinating mysteries are often found in the lives and hearts of its people.

In future books, you'll meet more of Sugarcreek's colorful residents, explore the treasures and secrets hidden within Rick's Attic, and perhaps discover, as Amy has, that sometimes the most unexpected discoveries lead us right where we need to be.

Thank you for joining me on this journey. I hope you'll stay for more Sugarcreek mysteries to come.

-Serena

SNEAK PEEK

SECRETS OF SUGARCREEK 2

SEARCHING FOR SAMUEL

The horse knew something was wrong before I did.

From my seat on the porch, I saw King—our lead Belgian—suddenly throw up his massive head and stop dead in his traces. His ears pricked toward the long gravel driveway. A moment later, Lucas, my farm manager, who had been walking behind the plow, stiffened, his hands tightening on the curved handles, his head cocked as he listened.

Then I heard it. Faintly at first. Then increasingly louder. A rapid drumming of hooves, urgent and fast, shattering the usual morning calm. A black buggy careened around the bend, its wheels spitting gravel. The horse pulling it was lathered in sweat, its sides heaving.

A young woman was at the reins, her voice carrying across the yard. *"Lucas! Komm schnell!"*

The raw desperation in her voice made the back of my neck prickle.

Trouble rarely announced itself so boldly among the rolling hills and whispered prayers of the quiet farming community of Sugarcreek, Ohio. I had been lost in my writing, but now my fingers froze above the keyboard. I hit save and rose to my feet.

The buggy jolted to a stop, and the woman vaulted out, hitting the ground running. Her dark dress whipped around her legs, her white prayer kapp askew.

Lucas anchored the plow, secured the reins, and ran to meet her. When they reached each other, she grabbed the front of his blue shirt with both hands, speaking rapidly in Pennsylvania Deutsch. Her words were sharp with panic.

The buggy horse shifted back and forth, harness jangling. In the back of the buggy, a little girl—no more than ten—noticed their horse's distress. She climbed into the front seat, took the reins, and murmured soothingly to the skittish horse. It settled under her gentle hand.

Two younger girls climbed forward to sit on either side of their sister. All wore light blue dresses, obviously made from the same bolt of fabric. They huddled next to her like little blue birds waiting out a storm. Their wide eyes locked on their mother.

I hesitated on the porch, torn between my ingrained New York City instinct to mind my own business and the urge to help. Here in Sugarcreek, people either ran toward trouble to lend a hand or popped a casserole into the oven to deliver later—depending on the situation. The one thing you didn't do, if you wanted to be part of this community, was nothing.

Since I very much wanted to be part of this community, I closed my laptop, stepped down off the porch, and went to see if I could help.

I recognized the woman now. Gretchen. Lucas's younger sister. I had met her briefly when she stopped by to leave off a birthday pie for her brother last month. It was his favorite, she said, grape.

As I crossed the yard, I mentally inventoried my kitchen. In Amish country, offering food and drink was always the right thing to do, no matter what sort of calamity might have struck.

"Excuse me," I said, approaching Lucas and Gretchen. "I have cookies and lemonade at the house if the children would like to come inside."

The girls turned toward me, their faces like small expectant sunflowers. They did not clamor or beg. Discipline ran deep here.

Lucas's gaze met mine, his blue eyes momentarily distant, as if he'd forgotten I existed. Whatever news Gretchen had brought had shaken him to the core.

Then his expression shifted—relief, perhaps, at knowing someone else was here to help shoulder the burden.

"*Danki*, Amy," he said, his voice steady with the quiet authority Amish men carried naturally. "*Die kinner* would probably appreciate it. But keep them on the porch where they can see their *mamm*."

Gretchen, visibly calmer, released her grip on her brother's shirt and turned to her daughters. "*Geh mit der Amy, meedlies. Sei brav.*"

I glanced at Lucas for translation.

"My sister told them to go with you and be good," he said.

The girls climbed down from the buggy, but the eldest first led the buggy horse to the trough and watched it drink thirstily. Her sense of responsibility and self-confidence was impressive. She knew the horse needed tending, even if the adults were too busy having a crisis to notice. Only after the horse was content, and she'd tied it to a post, did she take her sister's hands and accompany me to the porch.

None of them were wearing traditional prayer *kapps* over their braided, flaxen hair. This was highly unusual. Their mother must have been in a great hurry to have ignored it.

They were also barefoot, but that was normal. I winced when I saw them walking across the graveled driveway, but they didn't seem to notice. They were used to going barefoot except for church and sometimes trips to town.

I seated them at the picnic table on my porch, and they waited patiently as I brought a plate of sugar cookies out, and lemonade in paper cups.

"*Danki*," they chorused politely, daintily selecting one cookie each.

"I'm Amy," I said, settling across from them. "What's your names?"

The oldest girl straightened. "I am Sarah," she said, then gestured

193

to the others. "This is Ruth. She's five. And our baby sister is Laura. She's three."

"I'm glad to have you visiting."

"What is that?" Sarah pointed to my laptop, which I'd left sitting on an old table where I liked to write on nice days.

"It's my computer."

"What is it for?"

They had never seen a computer? These were not children who spent much time in Englisch houses.

"It is used for many things, but I write stories on it."

Sarah was less interested in the computer than the story-telling part.

"What kind of stories?"

"I mostly write stories about other people's lives."

Sarah stared at me for a good three seconds, as though mulling over my words.

"I tell stories to my sisters sometimes when they won't go to sleep," she said.

"I imagine they are wonderful stories," I said, with enthusiasm. I always try to encourage children who are budding story tellers.

"Probably not," she said. "They go to sleep very quickly once I start."

Laura gulped down her lemonade in a few swallows and held out her cup for more.

Sarah gave what sounded like a reprimand in Pennsylvania Deutsch. "*Nimm net zu viel!*"

"What did you say?" I asked.

"I told her not to drink so much."

"There's plenty," I assured her, refilling Laura's cup.

Sarah hesitated. "But Laura cannot always wait."

"Wait for what?"

"She is not long out of diapers. If she drinks too much, she wets herself."

The quiet confession hung between us. A child burdened with a woman's worries.

"If anyone needs the bathroom, it's just inside," I offered.

Sarah nodded solemnly. "*Danki*"

I changed the subject. "Is everything okay with your mother?"

"No." Sarah picked at her cookie. "Nothing is okay in our house now."

"Are you allowed to tell me why?"

She considered. "Our *Daett* is gone. *Mamm* doesn't know where he is."

"Your *Daett*?"

"Our father."

Little Laura reached for another cookie, but glanced first to see if it would be approved by her older sister. Sarah nodded, and Laura quickly snatched one up before her sister could change her mind. A few cookie crumbs clung to the sides of her tiny mouth.

"Has your mother called the police?"

"No." Like a little mother, Sarah wiped Laura's mouth with a napkin.

I would have loved to ask why no one had called the police, but it occurred to me I had already asked too much. It was not kind to interrogate children.

"Well," I said. "I hope your father comes back soon. Please help yourself to more cookies."

I saw Lucas and Gretchen approaching. His hand was cupping her elbow—a rare display of affection among the Amish. Gretchen forced a smile as she stepped onto the porch. "*Ach*, look at this *gude* party!"

Lucas met my eyes. "Can I speak with you inside?"

"Of course."

I could feel the children's worried eyes on me as Lucas and I stepped into the kitchen. I hoped he could help them. I knew one thing for certain from the few months I'd owned this farm—Lucas Hershberger would turn heaven and earth to help his family.

ALSO BY SERENA B. MILLER

SECRETS OF SUGARCREEK SERIES

- A Stranger for Christmas (Book 1)

LOVE'S JOURNEY IN SUGARCREEK SERIES

- The Sugar Haus Inn (Book 1)
- Rachel's Rescue (Book 2)
- Love Rekindled (Book 3)
- Bertha's Resolve (Book 4)
- The Heart of Sugarcreek (Book 5)

LOVE'S JOURNEY ON MANITOULIN ISLAND SERIES

- Moriah's Lighthouse (Book 1)
- Moriah's Fortress (Book 2)
- Moriah's Stronghold (Book 3)
- Eliza's Lighthouse (Book 4)
- Moriah's Lighthouse Collection (Books 1-3)

MICHIGAN NORTHWOODS HISTORICAL ROMANCE

- The Measure of Katie Calloway (Book 1)
- Under a Blackberry Moon (Book 2)
- A Promise to Love (Book 3)

UNCOMMON GRACE SERIES

- An Uncommon Grace (Book 1)
- Hidden Mercies (Book 2)
- Fearless Hope (Book 3)

ALSO BY SERENA B. MILLER

THE DOREEN SIZEMORE ADVENTURES

- Murder On The Texas Eagle (Book 1)
- Murder At The Buckstaff Bathhouse (Book 2)
- Murder At Slippery Slop Youth Camp (Book 3)
- Murder On The Mississippi Queen (Book 4)
- Murder On The Mystery Mansion (Book 5)
- Murder In Las Vegas (Book 6)
- Mystery At Little Faith Community Church (Book 7)
- Mystery At Alcatraz (Book 8)
- Murder In New York (Book 9)
- Murder In Egypt (Book 10)
- Murder In Sugarcreek (Book 11)
- The Accidental Adventures of Doreen Sizemore (Books 1-5 Collection)

APPALACHIAN HILLS

- A Way of Escape

NON-FICTION

- More Than Happy: The Wisdom of Amish Parenting

ABOUT THE AUTHOR

SERENA B. MILLER is a power-house in both publishing and television, earning her place as a *USA Today Bestselling Author* and collecting prestigious honors including the Romance Writers of America **RITA**, the American Christian Fiction Writers **CAROL**, and recognition as a **CHRISTY** Award finalist. Her signature storytelling first leaped from page to screen when *The Sugar Haus Inn* from her *Love's Journey in Sugarcreek* series became the award-winning UPTV movie *Love Finds You in Sugarcreek*, capturing the coveted **Templeton Epiphany Award**. Her mastery of heartfelt narratives has since inspired two acclaimed Hallmark Channel features: the compelling *An Uncommon Grace* and the captivating *Moriah's Lighthouse*, the latter drawn from her *Love's Journey on Manitoulin Island* series and set against the stunning backdrop of coastal France.

For More Information, Please visit serenabmiller.com

facebook.com/AuthorSerenaMiller

x.com/Serenabmiller

instagram.com/serenabmiller

amazon.com/author/serenabmiller

bookbub.com/authors/serena-b-miller

goodreads.com/SerenaBMiller